XENAKIS'S CONVENIENT BRIDE

BY

DANI COLLINS

MILLS
BOON

First published in Great Britain 2017
By Mills & Boon, an imprint of HarperCollins*Publishers*
1 London Bridge Street, London, SE1 9GF

Large Print edition 2017

© 2017 Dani Collins

ISBN: 978-0-263-07148-1

Printed and bound in Great Britain
by CPI Antony Rowe, Chippenham, Wiltshire

XENAKIS'S CONVENIENT BRIDE

The premise of an undercover billionaire was exciting all by itself, but when I found out I would be working with Rachael Thomas and Jennifer Hayward I was doubly thrilled. They are not just talented authors but wonderful people, and a joy to work with, so I dedicate this book to them with much affection and appreciation for their input.

I would be remiss, however, if I didn't include my husband. While we were brainstorming this story he helped me come up with the heroine's back story—specifically how cruelly Calli's father betrays her. As we bounced ideas back and forth, and the stakes went up, our voices grew louder and louder, causing our (grown) daughter to come into my office and ask with trepidation, "Are you guys fighting?" To be fair, I usually insist on complete silence while I work, so she had a right to be confused.

PROLOGUE

Stavros Xenakis threw his twenty-thousand-euro chips into the pot, less satisfied than he usually was postchallenge, but it had nothing to do with his fellow players or his lackluster hand.

His longtime friend Sebastien Atkinson had arranged his usual *après*-adrenaline festivities. It had wound down to the four of them, as it often did. Many turned out for these extreme sports events, but only Antonio Di Marcello and Alejandro Salazar had the same deep pockets Stavros and Sebastien did. Or the stones to bet at this level simply to stretch out a mellow evening.

Stavros wasn't the snob his grandfather was, but he didn't consider many his equal. These men were it and he enjoyed their company for that reason. Tonight was no exception. They were still high on today's exercise of cheating death, sipping 1946 Macallan while trading good-natured insults.

So why was he twitching with edginess?

He mentally reviewed today's paraski that had had him carving a steep line down a ski slope to a cliff's edge before rocketing into thin air, lifted by his chute for a thousand feet, guiding his path above a ridge, then hitting the lower slope for another run of hard turns before taking to the air again.

It had been as physically demanding as any challenge that had come before and was probably their most daredevil yet. Throughout most of it, he'd been completely in the moment—his version of meditating.

He had expected today to erase the frustration that had been dogging him, but it hadn't. He might have set it aside for a few hours, but this niggling irritation was back to grate at him.

Sebastien eyed him across the table, no doubt trying to determine if he was bluffing.

"How's your wife?" Stavros asked, more as a deflection, but also trying to divine how Sebastien could be *happily* married.

"Better company than you. Why are you so surly tonight?"

Was it obvious? He grimaced. "I haven't won

yet." He was among friends so he admitted the rest. "And my grandfather is threatening to disinherit me if I don't marry soon. I'd tell him to go to hell, but…"

"Your mother," Alejandro said.

"Exactly." They all knew his situation. He played ball with his grandfather for the sake of his mother and sisters. He couldn't walk away from his own inheritance when it would cost them theirs.

But "settle down?" His grandfather had been trying to fit Stavros into a box from the time he was twelve. Lately it had become a push toward picket fences. Demands he produce an heir and a spare.

Stavros couldn't buy into any of that so, yet again, he was in a power struggle with the old man. He usually got around being whipped down a particular path, but he hadn't yet found his alternate route. It chewed and chewed at him, especially when his grandfather was holding control of the family's pharmaceutical conglomerate hostage.

Stavros might be a hell-raiser, but his rogue personality had produced some of the biggest gains for Dýnami. He was more than ready to steer the ship. A wife and children were cargo he didn't need, but his grandfather seemed to think it would prove he was "mature" and "responsible."

Where his grandfather got the idea he wasn't either of those things, Stavros couldn't say. He upped his ante to a full hundred thousand, despite the fact his hand had not improved. He promptly lost it.

They played a little longer, then Sebastien asked, "Do you ever get the feeling we spend too much of our lives counting our money and chasing superficial thrills at the expense of something more meaningful?"

"You called it," Antonio said to Alejandro, tossing over a handful of chips. "Four drinks and he's philosophizing."

Sebastien gave Stavros a look of disgust as he also pushed some chips toward Alejandro's pile.

"I said three." Stavros shrugged without apology. "My losing streak continues."

"I'm serious." Sebastien was the only self-made billionaire among them, raised by a single mother on the dole in a country where bloodlines and titles were still more valuable than a bank balance. His few extra years of age and experience gave him the right to act as mentor. He wasn't afraid to offer his opinion and he was seldom wrong. They all listened when he spoke, but he did get flowery when he was in his cups. "At our level, it's numbers on a page. Points on a scoreboard. What does it contribute to our lives? Money doesn't buy happiness."

"It buys some nice substitutes." Antonio smirked.

Sebastien's mouth twisted. "Like your cars?" he mused, then flicked his glance to Alejandro. "Your private island? You don't even use that boat you're so proud of," he said, moving on to Stavros. "We buy expensive toys and play dangerous games, but does it enrich our lives? Feed our souls?"

"What are you suggesting?" Alejandro drawled, discarding a card and motioning for it to be replaced. "We go live with the Buddhists in the mountains? Learn the meaning of life? Renounce our worldly possessions to find inner clarity?"

Sebastien made a scoffing noise. "You three couldn't go two weeks without your wealth and family names to support you. Your gilded existence makes you blind to reality."

"Could you?" Stavros challenged, throwing away three cards. "Try telling us you would go back to when you were broke, before you made your fortune. Hungry isn't happy. That's why you're such a rich bastard now."

"As it happens, I've been thinking of donating half my fortune to charity, to start a global search-and-rescue fund. Not everyone has friends who will dig him out of an avalanche with their bare hands." Sebastien smiled, but the rest of them didn't.

Last year, Sebastien had nearly died during one of their challenges. Stavros still woke from nightmares of reliving those dark minutes. He'd wound up with frostbite burns on his fingers, but he'd been frantic to save Sebastien, unable to watch a man die again. A man whose life he valued. He felt sick recollecting it and took a sip of his whiskey to sear away the nausea.

"Are you serious?" Alejandro charged. "That's, what? Five billion?"

"You can't take it with you." Sebastien's shrug was nonchalant. "Monika is on board with it, but

I'm still debating. I'll tell you what." He leaned forward, mouth curling into the wicked grin he always wore when he proposed cliff diving or some other outrageous act. "You three go two weeks without your credit cards and I'll do it."

"Starting when? We all have responsibilities," Alejandro reminded.

After a considering pause, Sebastien canted his head. "Fair enough. Clear the decks at home. But be prepared for word from me—and two weeks in the real world."

"You're really going to wager half your fortune on a cakewalk of a challenge?" Alejandro said.

"If you'll put up your island. Your favorite toys?" He took in all three men. "I say where and when."

They all snorted with confidence.

"Easy," Stavros said, already anticipating the break from his grandfather's badgering. "Count me in."

CHAPTER ONE

Four and a half months later...

SHE FLOATED IN the pool on a giant ivory-colored clamshell, the pattern on her one-piece bathing suit a stark contrast of pink and green geometry against her golden, supple limbs. Her black hair spilled away from her face, a few tendrils drifting in the water. She wore sunglasses and red toe polish.

She was fast asleep.

As Stavros took in the way her suit painted her breasts and cut high over her hips, then smoothed over her mound to dip into the fork of her thighs, he stirred with desire. A detailed fantasy played out in his mind of diving in and coming up next to her, rolling her into his arms like an ancient god stealing a nymph and having her on that wicker sofa in the shade, behind the curtain of water on the far side of the pool.

The only sound in the high-walled courtyard was the patter of the thin waterfall. It poured off the edge of the ivy-entwined trellis that formed a roof over the lounge area and bar. The raining noise muffled his exhale as he set down the box containing power tools, a sledgehammer, trowels and adhesive compounds.

He stood and drank in another eyeful.

Perhaps being cast as a pool boy wasn't so bad after all.

Last night, he'd stood in a tiny, stuffy, *not* air-conditioned bachelor apartment cursing Sebastien with sincere vehemence.

His two-week challenge had started and his new "home" was a walk-up over a coffee-roasting operation. The smell was appalling. He couldn't decide which was worse: window open or closed. He had left it open while he compared his inventory of supplies with Antonio's photo from two weeks ago.

At least he'd had a heads-up from his friend as to what this challenge entailed. Given Antonio had been sent to Milan, Stavros had suspected he would be sent to Greece, and here he was.

Which had given Stavros a moment of pause.

He didn't care if he lost the boat, and even Sebastien's grand gesture was one he could make himself if it came right down to it. He had stepped off so many cliffs and platforms and airplanes at twenty-thousand feet, he shouldn't have hesitated to step off a ferry onto the island of his birth.

But he had.

Which made him feel like a coward.

He had forced himself to disembark and walk to his flat where he had discovered that, like Antonio, he had been provided a prehistoric cell phone and a stack of cash—two hundred euros. Lunch money. But where Antonio had been given a set of coveralls, Stavros had been given board shorts.

They were supposed to go two weeks without their wealth and reputation, but apparently his dignity had to be checked at the door, as well. At least his costume wasn't one of those banana hammocks so popular on European beaches. The uniform was tacky as hell regardless, pairing yellow-and-white-striped shorts with a yellow T-shirt.

Squinting one eye at the logo, Stavros had read the Greek letters as easily as he read English, and was offended in both languages. Zante Pool Care. Sebastien had told him to book vacation time, ensure his responsibilities were covered, then had sent him to work as a *pool boy*.

His phone was loaded with exactly three contacts: Sebastien, Antonio and Alejandro. He had texted Antonio a photo of his supplies along with the message, Is this for real?

If it turns out anything like mine, you're in for more surprises than that.

Antonio had discovered a son. How much more astonishing could it get?

If Stavros had a child living here, it would be a miracle. He'd left when he was twelve and had only kissed a girl at that point. Once he moved to America, high-risk behavior had become his norm. His virginity had been lost at fourteen to a senior at the private school he'd attended. She had favored black eyeliner and dark red lipstick—and young men with a keen interest in learning how to please a woman. Scrappers were her favorite and he'd been one of those, too.

A year later, he'd been making conquests of his grandfather's secretary and the nanny looking after his youngest sister. He wasn't proud of that, but he wasn't as regretful as he probably should be. Sex had been one of the few things to make him happy in those days.

Sex with that woman right there would certainly take the sting out of today's situation. The next *fourteen* days, in fact.

Another rush of misgiving went through him. This challenge was not a simple two weeks of pretending to be an everyman. Sebastien had left him a note.

You may remember our conversation last year, when you came to visit me as I was recovering from the avalanche. You opened that excellent bottle of fifty-year-old Scotch whiskey in my honor. I thank you again for that.

At the time you told me how losing your father had given you the strength to dig through the snow to save my life. Do you remember also telling me how much you resented your grandfather for taking you to New York and forcing you to answer to your American name? I suspect you were really saying that you didn't feel you deserved to be his heir.

Sebastien had chided Stavros for not appreciating his family and heritage, since Sebastien hadn't had those advantages. In his note, he continued:

I grant you your wish. For the next two weeks Steve Michaels, with all his riches and influence, does not exist. You are Stavros Xenakis and work for Zante Pool Care. Report at 6:00 a.m. tomorrow, three blocks down the road.

Antonio lasted two weeks without blowing his cover, so I have committed the first third of my five billion to the search-and-rescue foundation. Do the same, Stavros. It could save a life. And use this time to make peace with your past.

—Sebastien

Stavros had stayed up later than he should have, some of it jet lag, but mostly conjuring ways to get out of this challenge. Besides, he couldn't sleep in that hot room, tossing and turning on the hard single bed. Old-fashioned honor had him accepting his lot and falling asleep.

Then, even earlier than he needed to rise, the

sun had struck directly into his eyes. Large trucks with squeaky brakes had pulled in beneath the open window.

Disgusted, Stavros had eaten a bowl of dry cereal with the canned milk he'd been provided. He'd bought a coffee from a shop as he walked to "work."

His boss, Ionnes, had given him a clipboard that held a map, a handful of drawings and a work order. He had dangled a set of keys and pointed at a truck full of supplies and equipment, telling him to be sure to unload it since he wouldn't have the vehicle tomorrow.

Stavros might have booked a flight home at that point, but he had left his credit cards in New York, as instructed. He'd been completing Sebastien's challenges since his first year of university. None had killed him yet.

Nevertheless, as he'd followed the map, he had recognized the dip and roll of the road through the hills, eighteen years of changes notwithstanding. His heart had grown heavier with each mile, his lungs tighter.

Perhaps he wasn't defying his own death with

this challenge, but the loss of his father was even more difficult to confront.

He had sat in the driveway a full five minutes, pushing back dark memories by focusing on the changes in the home they'd occupied until their lives had overturned with the flip of a boat on the sea.

The villa was well tended, but modest by his current standards. It had been his mother's dream home when she married. She was a local girl from the fishing village on the bottom of the island. She had insisted her husband use this as his base. It had been a place where he could enjoy downtime. *Quality* time, with his children. She had called him a workaholic who was losing his roots, spending too much time in America, allowing the expanding interests of the family corporation to dominate his life.

The villa hadn't been new. It had needed repairs and his father had enlisted Stavros to set fresh paving stones at the front entrance while his mother and sisters had potted the bougainvillea that now bloomed in masses of pink against the white walls.

The memories were so sharp and painful as

Stavros sat there, he wanted to jam the truck in Reverse and get away from all of it.

But where would he go? Back to the blaming, shaming glint in his grandfather's hard stare? Back to the understudy role he hated, but played because his father wasn't there to be the star?

Cursing Sebastien afresh, Stavros glanced over his work order. He wasn't cleaning the pool, but repairing the cracked tiles around it. Déjà vu with paving stones. The mistress of the house would direct him.

He blew out a disgusted breath. After two decades of bearing up under his grandfather's dictates, and now facing a demand that he marry, he was at the end of his rope with being told what to do.

No one answered the doorbell so he let himself in through the gate at the side and went down the stairs into a white-walled courtyard that opened on one side to the view of the sea. His arrival didn't stir Venus from her slumber.

Damn, but his tension wanted an outlet. He let his gaze cruise over her stellar figure once more. If she was a wife, she was the trophy kind, but she wasn't wearing a ring.

The *mistress* of the place, his employer had said. He would just bet she was a mistress. How disappointing to have such a beauty reserved by his boss's client.

In another life, Stavros wouldn't have let that stop him from going after her.

This *was* another life, he recalled with a kick of his youthful recklessness.

Crouching, he scooped up a handful of water and flicked it at her.

The spatter of something against Calli's face startled her awake—in the pool, where she reflexively tried to sit up and immediately unbalanced. She tumbled sideways, sunglasses sliding off her nose, arms outstretched but catching at nothing. She plunged under the cold water into the blur of blue. Oh, that was a shock!

Ophelia.

Calli caught her bearings and pumped her arms to burst through the surface, sputtering, "You are so *grounded*. Go to your room."

But that wasn't Ophelia straightening to such a lofty height at the side of the pool. It was a conquering warrior, tall and forbidding, backlit by the sun so Calli's eyes watered as she tried to focus on him. His yellow T-shirt and shorts did nothing to detract from his powerful, intimidating form. In fact, his clothes clung like golden armor hammered across the contours of his shoulders and chest, accentuating the tan on his muscular biceps.

She couldn't see his eyes, but felt the weight of his gaze. It pushed her back and drew her forward at the same time, making her forget to breathe, making her hot despite being submerged to her shoulders and treading water.

Heat radiated through her, that dangerous heat that she had learned to ignore out of self-preservation. This time it wouldn't quash, which caused a knot of foreboding in her belly. He mesmerized her, holding her suspended as though in amber, snared into a moment of sexual fascination that seemed destined to last eternally.

He folded his arms, imperious, but his voice held a rasp of humor. "Lead the way."

To his room, he meant. It wasn't so much an invitation as an order.

She had the impression of a dark brow cocked

with silent laughter, which made her feel vulnerable. Not threatened, not physically, but imperiled at a deep level, where her ego resided. Where her fractured heart was tucked high on a shelf so no one could knock it to the floor again.

Her chest prickled with anxiety and she wiped her eyes, trying hard to see him properly, trying to figure out who he was and why he had such an instant, undeniable effect on her. His T-shirt sported the pool man's logo, but she'd never seen him before.

"I didn't hear you come in."

"Obviously. Up late?"

"Yes." It struck her very belatedly that it couldn't have been Ophelia to wake her. Calli had fallen asleep in the pool because she'd arrived home in the wee hours after leaving Ophelia at her maternal grandparents' home in Athens. She had driven half the night, then dozed in the car as she waited for the ferry.

Takis wasn't here. No one was except her and this barbarian of a man.

"I was traveling." She skimmed toward the stairs at the shallow end. "I knew workers were coming and didn't want to miss speaking to you by falling asleep inside. Where is Ionnes?"

"He gave me my assignment and told me I have two weeks."

"Yes, there's a party scheduled." The roll of alarm wouldn't leave her belly. It trebled when his shadow fell across her as she climbed the steps. He had plucked her filmy wrap from the chair and held it out for her like a gentleman.

He was *no* gentleman. She didn't know what he was, but had the distinct feeling he was *somebody*. Not a normal plebeian like her.

She took the wrap and struggled to push her wet arms into the loose sleeves. Why was she shaking? Oh, Ophelia had misguided taste! Why wasn't this wrap opaque? It was a birthday present and Calli had thought it delightfully feminine when she had opened it, but with the simple hook-and-eye closure over her navel, it was more provocation than cover, hanging open down her cleavage and parting in a slit over the tops of her thighs.

He noticed. He studied her from chin to toe polish, unabashed in the way he let his gaze move down and up, tightening her hair follicles inch by inch.

It wasn't the first time she'd been eyed up, but the locals knew she wasn't interested. Or considered her off-limits, at least. With tourists, she pretended she didn't speak English if she wanted to reject an advance.

Either way, it was always easy to brush men off, but not today. She *felt* his gaze. She told herself it was the water trickling off her, but that had never turned her inside out this way.

Once again she was accosted by defenselessness. Why? She'd been inoculated against men who used their looks to devastate.

Nevertheless, that's what he was. Devastatingly handsome. Standing on the same level with him didn't make him any less intimidating. He was big and powerful and now that she could properly see his face, she caught her breath in reaction. He wore a day's shadow of stubble and finger-combed hair, but those hollow cheeks and ebony brows were pure perfection. It wasn't the sculpted beauty of his face that arrested her, though. It was the fierce pride and unapologetic masculinity he projected.

It was the undisguised desire that flared in his black-coffee eyes as their gazes locked. The arrogant assumption he could *have*.

Because he knew she was reacting to him? Knowledge made his eyelids heavy while smug anticipation deepened the corners of his mouth.

She couldn't tear her eyes from his wide mouth, his lips brutally sensual, his jaw determined.

As he spoke, his voice lowered an octave to something that promised, yet warned. "Tell me what you want. I'm at your service."

Her body stung with a renewed flood of heat, countering the chill of her damp suit. *Please let him think the cold hardened my nipples.* But it was him. She knew it and he knew it and it scared her.

She scrambled back a step, trying to escape his aggressively sexual aura, and nearly stumbled into the pool.

He caught her by the arms, saving her from falling onto the steps under the water. It was chivalrous, but paralyzing, leaving her shaken. What was *wrong* with her?

She tried to lift her chin and look down her nose at him. "Let me go."

The amused heat in his brown eyes cooled to mahogany. "If that's what you want." He waited a beat, then lifted his hands away and straightened to his full height. "Watch your step."

He wasn't cautioning her about a slippery pool deck.

Her stomach wobbled and her heart pounded so hard she wanted to press her hand against her chest to calm it. She clenched her fist instead, swallowing to ease the dryness in her mouth.

"Your accent is strange." She narrowed in on that as a way to hold him at a distance. Something about his voice caused a prickle of apprehension in her. "Where are you from?"

His expression blanked into what must be a winning poker face. Which had to mean he was lying when he said, "I was born here."

"In Greece or on this island?" She knew most of the locals by sight, if not by name. "I don't recognize you. What's your name?"

A flash of something came and went in his gaze. Annoyance? "Stavros. I've lived abroad since I was twelve. I'm back for a working vacation."

She might have latched on to his lack of a surname if she hadn't just realized what colored his fluid Greek.

"You're *American*." On *vacation*.

Her blood stuttered to a halt in her veins, sending ice penetrating to her bones. No. Never again. No and no. She didn't care how good-looking he was. *No*.

As if he heard the indictment in her tone, he threw his head back, expression offended. "I'm *Greek*."

She knew her prejudice was exactly that. It wasn't even a real prejudice. She quite enjoyed chatting with rotund, married American tourists or any American woman. She wanted to *go* to America. New York, to be precise.

No, the only people she truly held in contempt were straight men who thought they could treat the local women like amusement-park rides. It didn't matter where they came from. Been there, done that, and her wounds were still open to prove it.

But the man who had left her with nothing, not even her reputation, happened to be American, so that was the crime she accused this one of committing.

"You're here to fix the pool," she reminded with a sharpness honed by life's hardest knocks. "You only have two weeks. Better get to it."

CHAPTER TWO

DAY THREE AND Stavros was sore. He worked out regularly, but not like this. After ten hours of physically breaking tiles with a sledgehammer and wheelbarrowing them *up* a flight of stairs, he had exchanged a few texts with Antonio. His friend's conglomerate built some of the world's tallest buildings.

Can I use a jackhammer?

He had included a photo.

I wouldn't. Could damage the integrity of the pool.

Stavros didn't have the cash to rent one anyway. If he rented anything, it would be a car. He had had to catch a lift with the coffee truck this morning and walk the rest of the way. What the hell did Sebastien think he would learn from this exercise?

Hell, it wasn't exercise. It was back-breaking labor. Which was allowing him to work out pent-up frustrations, but not the one eating a hole through him.

He wanted that woman. "Calli," she had informed him stiffly when he had asked for her name. She had pointed out the tiles that had been cracked by the roots of a tree. Since those tiles and that tree had to come out, they were redoing the entire surface surrounding the pool. *He* was.

She had disappeared into the house and had been a teasing peripheral presence ever since, flitting behind the screened door, playing music now and again, occasionally talking on the phone and cooking things that sent aromas out to further sharpen an appetite made ravenous by hard work.

He'd eaten well the first night, then did the math and realized he would have to make his own sandwiches the rest of his time here. It made the scent of garlic and oregano, lamb and peppers all the more maddening.

Who was she cooking for? It was ten o'clock in the morning and no one else was here, not even the man who kept her tucked away on the

Aegean like a holiday cottage. A married man, presumably.

Stavros couldn't quit thinking about that. Or the way she'd looked as she had risen like a goddess from the water. The physical attraction in that moment had been beyond his experience. He'd been compelled to move closer, had physically ached to touch her. His body still hummed with want and he had this nagging need to get back to that moment and pursue her.

But she had wished him dead on the spot. For being American.

It had been a slap in the face, not least because he had been working through mixed feelings over his identity for most of his life, ever since his father's father had yanked him from this paradisiacal island to the concrete one of Manhattan.

He'd always been too Greek for his grandfather's tastes and not Greek enough for his own. Having Calli draw attention to that stung.

Which left him even more determined to get back to that moment when she had revealed she desired him—*him*. Woman for man, all other considerations forgotten, most especially the man who kept her.

He hadn't experienced impotent rage like this since his early days of moving to New York, when he'd been forced to live a life he didn't want, yet defend it on the schoolyard. And he'd never before experienced such a singular need to prove something to a woman. Force her to acknowledge the spark between them.

He wanted to catch her by the arms, pull her in and kiss her until she succumbed to this fierce thing between them, *show* her—

He was too deep in thought, throwing too much weight behind the hammer. A chunk of broken tile flew up and grazed his shin, completely painless for a moment as it scored a lancing line into his flesh.

Then the burn arrived in a white-hot streak. He swore.

Calli heard several nasty curses in a biting tone. It meant trouble in any language.

She had spent the last few days trying to ignore Stavros, which was impossible, but she couldn't ignore *that*. She instinctively clicked off the burner and moved to glance through the screen-covered door to the courtyard.

He was bare-chested, wrapping his lower leg with his T-shirt. Blood stained through the bright yellow.

She ran for the first-aid kit, then hurried out to him. "What happened?"

It was obvious what had happened. He wore sturdy work boots and had showed up in jeans this morning, but it was already hot, even in the partially shaded courtyard and with the cooling curtain running beside the outdoor lounge. He had stripped down to his shorts an hour ago— yes, she had noticed—and now a jagged piece of tile had cut his leg.

"Let me see."

She started to open the kit, but as he unwrapped the shirt, she knew this was beyond her rudimentary skills. Good thing she wasn't squeamish.

"That needs stitches."

"Butterfly bandages will do."

"No, that's deep. It needs to be properly cleaned and dressed. Are your shots up-to-date?"

He gave her a pithy look. "I have regular physicals, and yes, I'm one hundred percent healthy."

She had a feeling he wasn't talking about tetanus, but refused to be sidetracked. For the last six years she'd been dealing with an overbearing boss and keeping his spoiled daughter out of trouble. She had learned to dig in her heels when circumstances required.

"Do you know where the clinic is? It's not a proper hospital and only open during the day. You're best to go now or you'll be paying the call-in fee for after hours. Or trying to find a boat to the mainland for treatment there."

She tried to ignore the twist and flex of his naked torso and the scent of his body as he reached to take a roll of gauze from the kit. "I don't have a vehicle."

"Shall I call your employer?"

"No one likes a tattletale." He efficiently re-wrapped the T-shirt and used the gauze to secure it, then used barbed clips to fasten the tails.

"No one likes stained tiles." She nodded at the red working its way through the layers of gauze. "I meant should I ask him to come take you to the clinic. I noticed you don't have the truck today."

"He'll say I have a job to finish. Which I do."

That was a barb at her, but he had been attacking his task doggedly, seeming determined to complete on time. Yes, she had peered out at him regularly, and his relentless work ethic dented her perception of him as a useless philanderer, intriguing her.

"Shall I drive you?"

"Look." He pinched the bridge of his nose, swore under his breath. "I don't have insurance. And I can't afford to pay for treatment. Okay?" He begrudged admitting it, she could tell. It wasn't so much a blow to his pride, though. He was impatient. Exasperated.

She was surprised. Not that he resented admitting he was short on resources, but that he was down on his luck at all. He didn't possess even a shred of humility and oozed a type of confidence she only saw in men with fountains of money, like Takis. Who *was* this man? What had happened to knock him off his keel?

"You think Ionnes will fire you if you make a work-injury claim? He's not like that. But I'll have them send the bill here. We can lump it in with the costs of the repair. My boss won't mind." Since she would pay it out of her own pocket.

She'd been at rock bottom once and Takis had saved her. She looked for chances to pay it forward. "I have to pick up a few groceries anyway."

That was another white lie and she wasn't sure why she tacked it on. Maybe to spare his pride because she knew what it was like to face losing self-esteem along with everything else.

Or because she wanted to spend time with this man, now her view of him was out of focus. She studied his stern visage only to have his attention narrow on her, like a predatory bird spotting an unsuspecting hare.

Why on earth had she thought he needed anything from her, least of all benevolence? That innate fierceness in his expression took him from handsome to all powerful. He was magnificent. She was spellbound, exactly as a bird's prey might be. Frozen in fascinated horror as she stared into her own demise.

"Your boss?" Sexual tension swooped in on the wings of a speculative look to perch between them, impossible to ignore.

Her scalp prickled and her breasts felt constrained by her bra. Who was she kidding? The sexual awareness had only dissipated because she'd been hiding in the house for three days. Had she realized he had made the same assumption about her as everyone else did she might have let the fallacy continue, since it offered a type of protection.

She wanted to be annoyed. Furious. Hurt.

She was scared. Her heart battered the inside of her rib cage like a fist against a wall. She needed protection because that youthful indiscretion that had put all the wrong thoughts into all the smallest minds was still alive in her. She had buried it deep behind the rarely used dishes, but he'd found it. He was reaching into her, bringing it to the light, blowing away the dust and asking, *What's this?*

With her stomach in knots and her blood moving like warm honey, she pretended ignorance. Indignation.

"Takis Karalis." She clumsily shoved the gauze and scissors back into the first-aid kit. "The owner of this villa. I'm his housekeeper. Why? What did you think?"

His gaze flicked over her, reassessing. It should have insulted her, but it caused a bright heat to glow inside her. She *wanted* him to discover that hidden part of her. Play with it. Polish it and make it shine.

In that moment, she wanted to be his type, able

to be casual about intimacy and physical delights. There was such promise in his eyes. Such pleasures untold.

But that way lay heartache of the most shattering kind. She knew it far too well. She had to remember that.

"You're not the first to think I'm his mistress." She hadn't bothered fighting the perception because her reputation had been in ruins the day Takis offered her this job. What was one more snide remark behind her back?

She needed to hold this man off, though, or she might self-destruct all over again.

"That's really sexist, you know, to assume that sleeping with the owner is the only reason I would be living here. Or to think I couldn't own this house. Not when it sounds as though I'm a lot closer to affording it than you are."

He didn't move, but his silence blasted her, warning her to mind herself.

A power struggle with this man was deeply foolish. In fact, trying to keep him at a distance might be a lost cause.

That thought was so disturbing, she could only blurt, "I'll meet you at the car."

She charged—retreated—into the house where she quickly scraped the moussaka filling she'd just finished browning into a bowl. She set it in the fridge before collecting her keys and purse, hands shaking.

Outside, her car was blocked by the pallet of new tiles he had unloaded a few days ago, along with the bin of broken ones.

Damn. No way could she risk staining the convertible. She glanced at his makeshift bandage. That must be painful, but he was stoic about it.

"We'll have to take the scooter." She moved to the stall and reached for her helmet, offering him Ophelia's. They were both pink, matching the Vespa.

"It's too small," he dismissed with a dry glance.

"I'm sure you're right. Your big head would never fit." *Shut up, Calli*. She set aside the helmet and paused before buckling on her own. "Do you want to go by yourself?"

"I don't know where the clinic is, do I? I might bleed out before I find it. No, by all means, take me."

He was being sarcastic, but his voice hit a velvety note with that last couple of words, causing a clench of heat in her. Her mind filled with imaginings she didn't even want to acknowledge. *Take me.* She maneuvered the scooter out of its spot with a practiced wangle, started it and balanced it between her legs.

He took up twice the space Ophelia did and wasn't shy about setting his hands on her hips. He guided her backside into a snug fit between his thighs.

She tried to stiffen and hold herself forward, but that only arched her tailbone into his groin. There was no escaping the surrounding heat off his bare, damp chest or rock-hard thighs shoved up against the outsides of hers. She wore shorts and a T-back sports cami. It was a lot of skin grazing skin. He let his hands fall to the tops of her legs, fingertips digging lightly into the crease at her hips.

She stopped breathing, held by an electrical current that stimulated all her pleasure points.

His growing beard of stubble scraped her bare shoulder and his breath heated the sensitive skin where her neck met her collarbone. "Shouldn't you be speeding off to save my life?"

"I'm seriously debating whether it's worth saving."

He hitched forward, jamming her buttocks even tighter into the notch of his spread legs.

She took off in a small act of desperation, glad for the muffle of the helmet and the buzz of the motor so she didn't hear his laugh, even though she felt it.

Honestly.

She sensed him turning his head this way and that as she took the shortcut over the top of the island, through the area with the very best views, between the extravagant mansions that dominated the peak of the hill. Then, as they came down the other side and the road wound toward the coast, the horizon appeared as a stark line between two shades of blue. They descended to where the land fell away in a steep cliff.

On the mountainside above them, stone fences kept sheep in their fields and hopefully off the roads. She kept her speed down just in case. The scent of blossoms in the lemon groves filled the morning air and she couldn't help relax as the cool breeze stroked over her skin.

His thumbs moved on her and she grew tense

in a different way. Tingles of anticipation raced up her rib cage, longing for his touch to rise and soothe, cup her aching breasts and draw her back into him more fully.

How did she even know what that would feel like enough to want it? Her sexuality had been flash frozen before it had had time to properly bloom. She didn't want to want a man's touch. It was self-destructive madness.

Descending the hairpin turns rocked her against him, driving her mad. She had come this way because it was quicker, but she usually avoided this route into the port town. It wasn't the once-daily ferry traffic and swarm of fresh tourists that bothered her. This part of the island actually had the best beaches and the better shopping. Ophelia begged to come here and there were a handful of really great restaurants.

Unfortunately, this route took her directly past a *kafenion* where local men sat and watched the world go by. Her father was often among them and she braced herself as they approached, refusing to look, keeping her nose pointed forward as she passed.

Not that he would acknowledge her, especially

with a man behind her. He would ignore her completely, exactly as she would ignore him. She just preferred not to set herself up for that blaze of layered pain.

They hit the melee of the village streets and she was glad they had the scooter. It allowed her to zigzag around traffic snarls and down narrow alleys, coming in the back way to the clinic where she parked next to staff cars.

"Who is Ophelia?" he asked as they dismounted.

"How—?" She followed his nod at the helmet she'd hung off the handlebars. "I forgot that was there." She rubbed the small, faded words she'd written across the back of her helmet shortly after Takis had bought the scooter. *Ophelia, stop that.*

Calli was only nine years older than the girl and didn't have any siblings. In a lot of ways, Ophelia felt like a little sister to her. In others, Calli's feelings went much deeper, more maternal. She adored the girl and was going to miss her terribly, even though Ophelia could be a complete brat at times.

"She's Takis's daughter. I look after her. Takis travels a lot, but she just turned fourteen and has convinced him to send her to boarding school.

She's with her grandparents, shopping for everything she'll need. She outgrew this island long ago."

Takis hadn't wanted to see it. Losing his wife had jaded him. He wanted to keep his daughter sheltered as long as possible. Unfortunately, that had meant the girl had chafed and acted out—for Calli, thanks very much.

He was finally allowing the girl to spread her wings, though, which loosened the complex grip of gratitude and genuine love that had kept Calli here, raising a child who needed her while yearning to find her own.

"So you're a nanny." He said it like he didn't believe it.

"Hmm? Oh. Yes. Nanny, housekeeper, party planner. Whatever Takis needs me to be." She started toward the clinic. "Barring what you suggested earlier."

"Good." He moved quicker than her, catching at the door to hold it for her, filling her vision with his contoured chest lightly sprinkled with fine black hair, his skin burnished bronze, his nipples dark brown. "I'm glad you're single."

"I intend to stay that way." Her voice husked despite her attempt to sound haughty.

"Even better."

A pained fist clenched behind her breastbone. *Vacation. Playboy.* She flipped her hair as she passed him. "I should have given you one of Takis's old shirts. I'll buy you something from the shop across the road. After I make arrangements to pay your bill."

Stavros walked outside, pocketing a course of precautionary antibiotics, rolling his eyes at the primitive concoction he'd been given. He might have pointed out the far more effective class that had recently passed approval if he hadn't already been skating so close to revealing his identity.

As he had wrapped his injury, he had realized he couldn't use the global health insurance that covered Steve Michaels, heir to a multinational pharmaceutical corporation. Using his Greek surname for the admission form had been another gamble. The nurse, a woman approaching retirement, had eyed him, saying she had attended school with a local woman who had married a Stavros Xenakis. Any relation?

He had ducked raking over the past. It promised to be a lot worse than this dull ache in his shin. Besides, Antonio had managed to get through two weeks without blowing his cover. Stavros's ego refused to fail where his friend had succeeded.

He spotted Calli standing in the shade near the Vespa. As he approached, her gaze took an admiring sweep over his still-naked torso, betraying that her disdain for him was an act even as she shook out a T-shirt and offered it to him with an expression on her face like an offended matron's.

The shirt was imprinted with a subtle design of the Greek flag in stripes of white against the blue of the shirt, which was something he might have chosen for himself if he wore T-shirts with logos.

"I expected 'Greece' is the word."

"I almost got the one that said 'Made on Mount Olympus,' but, you know, why state the obvious?"

"Careful, Calli. That sounds like you find me attractive." He shrugged on the shirt, telling himself it was his competitive nature that made him provoke her. Pursue her. She was a *nanny*, for God's sake. One who was snobbishly turning down the pool boy. That made her an amusing distraction, not someone worth obsessing about.

"Keep telling yourself that." She turned to reach for her helmet.

"*You* are telling me." He caught her arm, waiting for her gaze to flash up to his. "Every time you look at me." He demonstrated by taking her other arm and gently pressing her elbows back, giving her plenty of opportunity to recoil, but she didn't, not even when her breasts nudged his chest.

She caught her breath and set tense fingers on the sides of his rib cage, even notched her chin in a signal of defiance, but she didn't tell him to stop. A fine quiver made her lashes tremble. Her pulse fluttered in her throat and she searched his gaze for his intention, but she wasn't afraid. She was excited.

She was daring him.

This was why he was obsessing. A primitive, powerful hunger rose in him, answering the siren song she was singing.

"I know the signs of desire in a woman." He looked down at where her nipples were hard beneath the soft cups of her bra. He wanted to bite at them through the fabric. "They're painted all over you. Just as I'm sure you felt me hard against your ass the entire ride down here. We react to each other. Why fight it?"

He was hard again, steely and aching as he watched her lips part. His ears buzzed, awaiting her words, but she only let panting breaths whisper between them.

The compulsion to plunder her mouth nearly undid him, but he tasted the side of her neck first, liking the tiny cry of surprise that escaped her as he ran his hot tongue over salty skin that smelled of coconut and lavender. He delicately sucked, then nibbled his way up her neck. She melted with each incremental bite of his lips against her skin.

By the time he got to her mouth, she was making a delicious noise of helplessness, leaning her body into his, breasts pressing in soft cushions against his chest. Her lips were as plump and responsive as any he'd ever tasted. More. He was starving. Rapacious. She'd been driving him crazy, invading his dreams every night and now, finally, she was his.

Releasing her arms, he let one hand trail down

to cup her ass and draw her soft belly into the ache pulsing between his thighs. His other hand went into her hair, tugging to pull her head back so he could feast on her throat again, loving the way it made her knees weaken so she twined her arms around his neck and hung helplessly against him, mons pushed against his straining erection.

He wanted to back her into the shade and take her against the wall of the clinic, but he could hear a car crunching on the gravel as it entered the lot behind them. He forced himself to lift his head and waited for her heavy eyelids to blink open, for her honey-gold eyes to focus.

"Did you want to make another remark about my finances now, to put me in my place?" He kept his tone light, but he never let anyone get away with insulting him. Screw Sebastien's challenge. He was still a man and he wasn't a weak one.

She paled beneath her golden tan and pushed out of his arms, gaze dropping with shame. "This was a punishment? Well, didn't you teach me."

The scrape of bitterness in her tone dug like talons into his gut. She covered her glossy black hair with the helmet, avoiding his gaze, but he could see her thick lashes moving in rapid blinks.

He was used to sophisticated women who made the most of their attraction and offered themselves without ceremony. Lately, since his grandfather's wish that he marry had become known, there had been an even bigger frenzy of pretty piranhas circling and luring, promising any carnal act he requested if he would only put a ring on a finger.

This one stood before him with her bare, fraught expression and mouth still pouted by their kiss, wearing an unassuming wardrobe over a body that looked fit from sporty exercise, rather than sculpted by starving herself and bankrolling a plastic surgeon. When she had kissed him back, it hadn't been the toying provocation of a woman trying to lead a man by his organ. She'd been hot and wanton, completely swept away—as he had almost been.

He put his hand on her flat stomach, urging her to pause and look at him. "I kissed you because I wanted to."

"You kissed me because you thought you were entitled to." She snapped the buckle under her chin. "I knew what kind of man you were the day we met." She grasped his finger, disdainfully peeling his hand away from her abdomen and discarding it. "I forgot once, but I won't make that mistake again."

"American?" The contempt curling her lips went into him like a blade, even sharper than the first time. "Not Greek enough for you?"

"A tomcat. Here for a good time, not a long time."

Calli caught sight of a car, *not* her mother's, but close enough to make her take the opposite direction out of town, not wanting to pass her father's end again.

Besides, she found the southern end of the island more peaceful. Fishermen launched their small boats and grape growers eked out a living from the dry, rocky land. It was very desolate, but also very Greek. It was home.

She loved this island. She had stayed after her father threw her out for many reasons, money being the big one, at least at first. She hadn't had the means to get off the island, let alone to New

York, and hadn't wanted to be exiled from her home along with losing everything else.

She hadn't wanted to leave until she could go to America, but no matter how she tried, those goalposts kept moving. Takis had even tried to help her, but that had fallen apart. Meanwhile, he gave her a better job than anyone with her limited skill set could expect. The longer she stayed, the deeper her ties to him and Ophelia grew, rooting her here even more.

Staying had been a statement of defiance, too, as much as a lack of choice. Her father thought she had shamed him? So be it. She had stayed and lived in what appeared to be flagrant sin with a man much older than herself, continuing to shame him. He deserved to feel ashamed. She would never forget what he had done to her and her son. She wanted him to know it.

But soon she would have to say goodbye and make her way to New York. Once Ophelia left, Calli planned to leave, too.

She was terrified.

"He's in a better place," her mother had said, two days after Dorian was gone, when Calli had caught up to her at one of her cleaning jobs.

"Stop saying that! *He's not dead.*"

Her father could shout that lie until he was blue in the face, but Calli *knew*. Brandon's parents had offered her money to hand over the baby, claiming they had a nice family who would raise him to their standards, but she had to give up all claim to him. She had refused.

Then suddenly Dorian was gone and she knew, didn't have proof but she *knew* her father had taken the money and sold her son to them.

"Why are you doing this?" she had cried at her mother. "Why are you letting him get away with it?" It was more frankness than had ever passed between them, so many things always left unsaid to keep the peace.

"Look at you!" Her mother had turned on her with uncharacteristic sharpness. "You're a child. One turned willful and wild. What kind of mother would you make? And you want to bring up your baby in *this*?" She'd showed no pity as she waved at Calli's swollen eye and cut lip, the bruises on her shoulders and back, the dirt clinging to her clothes and hair from sleeping on the beach.

It was true she didn't want her son raised under

the heavy hand of a hard, angry man like her father. She had learned an even uglier rage lived in him than she had ever feared or imagined.

"I'm going after him," she had declared.

"Don't. Those are powerful people, Calli. They can offer more, but they can *take* more. *He is in a better place.* Accept it."

"What kind of mother are *you* to say that to me?" Calli had ducked the scrub brush that came flying at her, then had run out of the house to avoid a fresh beating on top of the one still throbbing black-and-blue under her skin.

She had numbly retraced this long stretch of ragged coastline on foot after leaving that stranger's house, fighting her mother's words. Calli had been a good mother, for the short time she'd been allowed to try.

But she'd been young enough to still put stock in the words of those who were older, those who seemed to know better. As she was forced into more and more desperate decisions simply to stay alive, she had started to wonder if her mother wasn't right. She was a terrible person. Not fit to be a mother.

Now it was six years later and she had tried

several times to locate her son, but things had happened to prevent her. Each small failure had reinforced that she wasn't meant to have him.

He *was* in a better place without her.

But she would never rest until she knew that for sure.

It made moments like this bittersweet. As the road quieted and the cool, salt-scented air swept over her, she drank it in, trying to relax and live in the moment. To accept life's hard turns and just be.

But that made her hyperaware of Stavros's strong frame surrounding her.

It made her remember their kiss.

Think of Brandon.

That memory was a distant recollection of flattery and pretty lies that she had believed because she had wanted to. Those first stirrings of attraction were nothing compared to the way this man's aura glowed off him and sank through her skin, slanting rosy hues through her without even trying. He set her alight in ways she hadn't believed were possible.

She told herself the vibration of the bike caused her nipples to feel tight and her loins to clench in hollow need. She was hot because it was a hot summer day. She was flush against the front of his hot body while the hot sun beat down.

Still, it was all she could do to stop herself from inching back into the hard shape pressed to her butt. She knew what it was and it provoked an ache into her breasts and belly and the juncture of her thighs. It was maddening.

She told herself not to give him this power over her, but it wasn't voluntary. It simply *was*.

And now she was forced to slow and extend this ride. Up ahead, the road was plugged with sheep, the herd thick between the thornbush-covered hillside and the rail that kept traffic from dropping off the short, sharp ledge to the scrub-covered shoreline.

On impulse, she made a sharp right onto the narrow peninsula that jutted out into the sea. Might as well be a decent hostess if they were right here. At least she could take a break from the physical contact.

Behind her, Stavros said something, a curse or a protest, she wasn't sure. His hands seemed to harden on her hips, fingertips digging in, but not in a sensual way.

Worried about getting back to work?

"The sheep will be twenty minutes clearing the road. It would take that long to go back around the other way," she called back as she wound along the goat track to the end.

The motion rubbed their bodies together even more and she was relieved to finally stop the bike and climb off. "At least there's a breeze out here. And it's pretty."

It was spectacular. The jut of land provided a near 360-degree view of the horizon. As she took off her helmet, there was no sound except the whisper of wind in the long grass and the rush of foaming waves against the boulders that formed the tip of the spit.

The rugged beauty was deceptive, though. Sometimes people walked out on those boulders, tourists who didn't know better. One slip could be deadly. The currents were dangerous and if bad weather was headed for the island, it showed up here first, chopping the sea into crashing waves, then throwing itself against the land in mighty gusts and nasty pelts of rain.

When Stavros stayed by the bike, she glanced back. "Is your leg bothering you?"

He sent her a filthy look, one loaded with resentment and hostility, taking her aback.

She parted her lips, not knowing what to say.

The way he stalked behind her, toward the tip of the spit, had her stammering, "You can't swim here. It's too dangerous. People die."

"I know." The gravel in his voice made her scalp prickle.

Stavros paused where the end of the striated rock had been broken off by a millennia of waves, the pieces left jagged and toppled in the churning water below.

Part of her had disbelieved that he had ever lived here, but as he looked out as if he saw something in the rolling, shifting sea, she had the impression he had stood in that exact spot before. Searching.

Her heart dropped.

He seemed very isolated in that moment, with his profile stark and carved, his hands slowly clenching as though he was bearing up under tortuous pressure.

His anguish was palpable.

She moved without consciously deciding to,

standing next to him, searching his expression, wanting to reach out and offer comfort.

His flinty gaze seemed to drill a hole into the water, one that led directly to the underworld. He looked as though he was girding himself to dive straight into it.

His ravaged face made her throat sting. His posture was braced and resolute. Like he was taking a lashing, but refused to cringe. He accepted the castigation. Bore it, even though there was no end in sight for this particular punishment.

A clench of compassion gripped her, but he was a column of contained emotion.

"Stavros." It was barely a whisper. She wanted to say she was sorry. How could she have known this would be so painful for him?

His face spasmed before he hardened his jaw and controlled his expression. When he cut his gaze to hers, it was icy cold. His voice was thick with self-contempt.

"Man whore is the least of my character flaws."

Her heart lurched. She knew how deeply that word *whore* cut. She hadn't meant to sink to that level when she had called him a tomcat.

In that moment, she knew he was nothing like

superficial Brandon who threw money at an un-planned child to make it go away. Stavros was as deep as the vast sea they faced, churning beneath the gilded surface he presented to the world.

"I didn't know—" She touched his cold arm, but he shrugged off her light fingers.

"Let's go. I have a job to finish so I can get the hell off this island."

CHAPTER THREE

THE WATER CURTAIN had been only a drawing and some footings when his father had died. Stavros was laying the tiles around the base of the two columns, standing back to assess his work, when Calli spoke.

"I've been making spanakopita. I thought you might like some."

He'd been trying to keep her at a distance these last few days, feeling exposed since she had blithely forced him to face what he had been avoiding for twenty years.

Swim for shore. I'll be right behind you.

He had always had a defiant streak. He came by it honestly. His father had flouted rules just as often.

Why do I have to wear a life vest if you don't? he had asked his father as they'd boarded the small skiff.

Do you want to go fishing or not? I'll be fine. Put on your vest or we're not going anywhere.

Sebastien had asked Stavros why he owned a boat he didn't use. That was why. Boating made him sick and it wasn't *mal de mer*.

He'd always had it in his mind that he would overcome that weakness, though. Perhaps he would even sail these waters one day.

To what end? So he could do this? Relive the day he had, for once, done as he had been told and swam? Swam as if his life depended on it, because it had?

While abandoning his father to his death.

He kept thinking that Sebastien could have the damned yacht. He didn't want it. It certainly didn't bring him any sort of happiness, exactly as Sebastien had called it that night in St. Moritz.

He should have helped his father get to shore. That was the voice he used money and toys and women and death-defying feats to muffle. It wasn't only his opinion. That truth had been reinforced in his grandfather's interrogation after the accident and colored every word his grandfather had spoken to him since.

Use your American name. It's better for busi-

ness. Translation: "You don't have the right to use Stavros. That was your father's name."

You want the company to succeed, don't you? Don't let your father's dreams die with him.

Think of your mother and sisters. Do you want them to be well supported or not? It's up to you.

Basically, "do as I say or I will turn all of you onto the street."

Despite Stavros saying nothing to Calli about the way his father had been killed, she had offered a doe-eyed empathy that had been too tender a thing to bear. He had brought her back here and worked until dark, only pausing when she had brought out a plate of ground lamb sprinkled over triangles of grilled pita, and a dollop of *tzatziki* with a salad of peppers.

"I'll have to start over with the moussaka tomorrow, but no sense letting this go to waste," she had said.

She was acting compassionate when he had only ever seen grief in his mother and sisters and that well-deserved censure from his grandfather.

Yet, since that day on the spit, he hadn't been dwelling on the accident so much as how his grandfather had yanked them off this island and sold the house immediately after the accident. He had changed their names and refused to hear Greek under his roof, denying Stavros this connection to his roots. To his memories of a happy childhood.

"Keep the keys for the Vespa," Calli had told Stavros when he finished up that evening. "If I need it, I'll let you know."

Her generosity had been hard to assimilate against the criticism that had dominated his life for nearly two decades. He had taken the keys, but turned from her kindness like it was too hot, too bright.

He had worked half days on the weekend, spending the afternoons reacquainting with the island, allowing himself to remember more than his fatal mistake, all the while trying *not* to wish her curves were spooned against his back. He didn't need a woman cuddling him through this. He had to face it alone.

He had come to a decision among the seared hills and unforgiving water. He wasn't a boy any longer and his grandfather would no longer be his master. He would buy back his former home,

if only to have somewhere to go when his grandfather made good on his promise to cut him off.

The decision eased the turmoil in him, put a
fire in his belly. Put him in a conquering mood
as he eyed the woman who moved with such un-
conscious grace. Her loose hair swung as she set
the plate of triangular pastries on the low table
next to the lounger. Her peach-colored shorts
hugged her perfect ass and her breasts moved
freely under her sleeveless pink top. The tails of
the shirt were knotted above her navel, exposing
a strip of skin he instantly wanted to touch. Taste.

He wanted her, wanted to lose himself in her.
He wanted to imprint himself on her as if he
could imprint himself on this island with the action. As if he could become the man he should
have been by conquering *her.*

While she wanted to stroke his hair and say,
"There, there."

He moved to the sink in the wet bar and washed
his hands, shaking them dry as he said, "Quit
feeling sorry for me."

She blinked. "I don't."

"What are you out here for, then?"

"I thought you might be hungry."

"I am." He advanced on her, watching her eyes widen. "But not for food." A small lie. He was starving and broke after using the wages he had been given last Friday to pay her back for the stitches. "No appetite for charity, either."

Calli scented danger, but held her ground.

"I'm just being nice." He'd been so haunted on the point. It had hurt her to see it. She knew what it was like to grieve and hate yourself. She struggled with it daily and she was facing it anew, not wanting to be so fascinated by him, tortured by their kiss, writhing every night on her sheets, caught in the grip of physical infatuation.

We react to each other. Why fight it?

Was it really the same for him? She searched his expression for the man who had seemed so human that day. So steeped in pain.

"You can talk to me, is all I'm saying."

His laugh held an edge that cut past her gentle tone to tighten her throat around any further offers of sympathy. "I don't want to talk. I want *you.*"

She blushed, stung, while he kept coming forward. She backed up until she came to the wall of the courtyard, between the end of the lounger and the corner of the wet bar. His hands planted on either side of her head and she was trapped.

Her heart battered her rib cage, but her fear was the exhilarated kind.

He wasn't a spoiled rich boy like Brandon. Maybe she didn't know much about him, but she knew he was a man who understood regret and paid his debts and knew his own worth was intrinsic, not contained in a bank balance.

He also didn't lie and say he loved her. He looked her in the eye and spoke the truth. *I want you.*

An answering want had been pulling at her like a tide from the moment she'd seen him. She succumbed before he even touched her, letting her head rest against the wall and her lips part as she regarded him from beneath eyelids that grew heavy between one breath and the next.

Exultation flashed in his expression and he crowded closer, hot, damp hands finding the bare skin between her shirt and shorts.

The burning sensation was so acute, the electricity in his touch so sharp, she jerked in reaction.

His hands firmed, as though he was pinning

her. Controlling her. He was. She was at his mercy. A distant voice in her head screamed that this was perilous, but there was pain deep down in her and she suspected he could soothe it. There was an ache in him, too, one that she longed to ease.

She was, after all, only human. They understood each other on a subliminal level. That was what she kept telling herself.

As he lowered his head, she slid her hands across his jaw. His stubble had softened as it grew in. She buried her fingers into the short, thick strands of his hair.

He took her mouth with ruthless command, stabbing his tongue and sliding his lips against hers with carnal passion.

It might have struck her as an abrupt shove into too much intimacy, but she'd spent the weekend reliving their kiss outside the clinic. Having the real thing, his taste of midnight and mystery on her tongue, his magnificent torso shifting against her, his knowing hands sliding up beneath her top to cup the undersides of her breasts, plunged her into a delirium of want. She wasn't wearing a bra and her nipples stung with longing, alert and needy, yearning for his touch, waiting.

He slid his knee between hers, positioned his hard thighs against the insides of hers to open her, then let her feel the hard ridge of his erection against the tender flesh pulsing between her legs. His thumbs swept across her nipples at the same time.

She shuddered at the onslaught of sensation, moaning into his mouth. Heat poured into the place where he rocked, making each of his mock thrusts that much more powerful. It was raw and raunchy, yet stoked such a white-hot fire in her she went blind with it.

She turned melty and shivery at the same time and kissed him back with a wild lack of inhibition or even skill. Pure reaction. The burn in her raged higher, engulfing her, threatening to slip beyond her control.

Clenching her fists in his hair, she dragged his head up, gasping, "I'm not on the Pill. I don't want to get pregnant."

"You don't get pregnant from this, *koukla mou.*" He kept up the abbreviated thrust of his pelvis against hers, and stole one of her hands from his hair to pin it to the wall above her head. His fingers curled into hers, thick enough to cause a little stretch between them as he dipped his mouth to her neck.

Her skin tingled under the hot suck of his lips. He splayed his other hand over her naked breast under her shirt. Her flesh felt swollen and hard. His palm abraded her nipple. Glittering lines of sensation shot into her abdomen and lower.

Her hips bucked of their own accord, answering his movements, seeking that hard, hard ridge against the bundle of nerves pulled so tight she couldn't bear it. So close. So hot. So tense. She felt as though she'd been ignoring thirst and suddenly, here was the water, promising a quench that was a type of absolution. She needed it, needed more of him. *Needed that*, the elusive thing hovering just out of reach, closer, nearly in her grasp.

She tightened her hand in his, urging him with her grinding hips. Begging.

She wasn't really letting this happen right here, against a wall, behind a rush of water with a man she barely knew, was she? Was she?

Oh, yes. She *was*.

Release struck in a flash of heat and a rush of shivery joy. She lost herself to the moment, falling apart, soaring and flying. She might have fallen down if not held in place by his strength and the hard pin of his weight and that relentless press of his hips that shot sensation through her again and again.

Distantly she realized she was making animalistic noises. Her free hand went to his lower back, encouraging his dying movements while he cupped her jaw and set nibbling kisses against the corners of her panting mouth, saying, "Beautiful. So gorgeous." His tongue slid against her bottom lip like he was taking a final taste of an excellent meal. His body was so tense he quivered with strain. The heady fragrance of male sweat surrounded her, sexy and compelling.

She felt drugged. Her breath was uneven, her pulse fluttering. She couldn't believe he had done that to her, fully clothed. Or that she was still so aroused. If anything her skin was more sensitized and desperate for his touch, her loins even more achy with want.

She opened her eyes and looked into the earthy brown of his, read desire, but humor, too. He wasn't as lost to passion as she was.

It was a blow. Even more of one when he said, "Are you a virgin?"

"I know *that's* not how you get pregnant!" She gave him a shove, but he barely moved. His thick, aroused flesh sat against her tingling mound, only the thin layer of his board shorts and the seam of her cotton ones between. "I thought you were as caught up as I was and might try to…" Her voice dried up. She had to strain to find sound again. "Apparently not."

She gave him another shove, not caring how good he'd made her feel physically. She wouldn't forgive him for playing with her like a toy.

He only cupped her throat, thumb moving with lazy eroticism beneath her ear while he told her in explicit detail what he wanted to do to her. "But I don't have a condom, so we'll have to find other ways to appease ourselves, won't we?"

His eyes were nearly black, they were so dark. His mouth held a line of wicked intent that bordered on cruel. But his kiss was tender and incredibly sweet after the storm of sensuality she'd endured. Her lips clung to his, encouraging him to linger. Inviting him. Capitulating…

The scrape of the screen door into the house

sounded and a male voice called, "Calli." It was an equally harsh scrape across her nerve endings.

Stavros drew back enough to frown. "Who's that?"

"Takis." She looked past his shoulder, through the blur of the curtain, to see Takis pause outside the door as though looking for her. She pushed at Stavros.

He didn't move. "Get rid of him."

Seriously? "He's my boss."

Stavros glared at her, backed off enough to glance down to where his shorts were tented and bit out a dissatisfied curse.

He threw himself through the thin waterfall into the pool.

Stavros came to the surface in time to see a flustered Calli moving toward a silver-haired man in a suit. He kissed her cheek, but it was a distracted greeting. His frowning gaze lingered on her blushing face before fixing on Stavros with open hostility.

"Who is that?"

"Stavros. He's fixing the tiles."

"From the water?"

It was a singular experience for Stavros to be spoken *about* when he was right here, listening, especially in such a dismayed, dismissive fashion. Like he wasn't good enough to be in this man's world, let alone his pool.

The denigration was enough to cool his ardor, but made him want to laugh at the same time. *Do you know who I am?*

Takis probably regarded himself as quite wealthy and powerful, but he would very soon be selling this country cabin to Stavros for what amounted to pocket change.

There was more that Stavros instantly disliked. The man kept his arm looped around Calli's waist as he watched Stavros climb from the pool.

Whatever he needs me to be.

A surge of something ripped through Stavros. Jealous rage? The thought scored a direct hit in a way the condescension hadn't.

He reacted reflexively, walking tall as he approached, shoulders set, oblivious to the water sluicing off his sopping T-shirt and shorts, puddling with each footstep as he advanced, about to go on the attack. Eager for it.

He was not only the heir to a fortune, but the

bold, innovative president of a multinational corporation who had exponentially increased the reach and value of that entity into the stratosphere. In becoming *that* man, he had learned to exert his will over a tyrant whose autocratic nature matched his own. Nothing held him back. Nothing was unattainable. Men like Takis weren't even breakfast. They were a protein bar washed down with a swish of water on the way to a morning workout.

A frown of alarm pulled between Calli's brows, like she wasn't sure she recognized him.

In that second, he remembered the bet. Five more days of playing pool boy. He bit back an imprecation.

No matter which guise he wore, Stavros Xenakis was no lame quitter, but he wasn't about to bow and scrape before Calli's boss. Or pretend that Calli was anything except his. Takis could delude himself all he wanted. She had fallen apart against *him*.

Stavros conveyed that message as he extended his hand.

"Takis. Nice to meet you. Thanks for the dip. I needed to cool off." He let his gaze cut to Calli's, allowing them both to see he was remembering how she had climaxed from merely the tease of sex. How would she react when they were naked and he was inside her? Would she scream?

She blushed ferociously. "I'll leave you to show Takis your work," she choked. "Coffee?" she offered her boss.

"Thank you." He released her, face hard, eyes diamond sharp.

Takis didn't say much as he took in the work Stavros had completed thus far. The broken tiles were gone, Ionnes having removed the bin from the front late last week. Since then, Stavros had been laying the new ones, and he was taking as much care and pride as he would if the house were his own. He had already sent a text to Antonio, asking him to arrange an agent to appraise the house since he couldn't contact his own.

Takis went into the house and Stavros went back to work, chafing at the need to be patient. He was coming down the outer stairs with a load of tiles when he overheard voices through the small, shutter-covered window above him.

"—damned sure he's not a tile layer by trade, so who is he?"

"Ionnes wouldn't send anyone he didn't trust." Something snapped, like a towel. Calli, folding laundry perhaps. "If you have concerns, tell me and I'll relay them."

"My concern is that you were kissing him."

Stavros set down the tiles with care, straightening to scowl at the window.

"Are you sleeping with him? You are." The accusation held dismay. "I can see it in your face."

"I am not! And it's none of your business if I was. Do I ask you why your shirts smell like perfume?"

"He's a womanizer—"

"I know what he is." The words burst out in a hot voice. "I know he's only here on vacation, but there's more to him than that."

"I'm sure there is, but whatever it is, you haven't seen it. What happened to waiting until you married?"

"I said that for Ophelia's sake."

"You said that to *me*. And I did offer to marry you."

The green haze returned to Stavros's vision. His chest grew tight.

"Takis—"

"I'm not asking again," he said impatiently. "I'm past wanting more children myself. But I expect you to shoot higher than a pool boy, Calli. You'll starve. Is it because he's American? I've told you, if you want to visit New York, I'll take you."

"I need more than— That's not why— Do you think I want to feel this way?" Something slammed, like the door on a washer. "About someone only passing through? But maybe I could do with a conquest, too. Did you think of that?"

"No." The word was flat and hard. "That is the furthest thing from who you are. He is a walk down a path you've already traveled. Learn from your mistakes…"

Their voices faded and Stavros picked up the tiles. He would have been amused by the blatant snobbery if it didn't sound so much like his grandfather.

Show me you're capable of looking to the future. Find someone worthy of carrying on our name.

Their *American* name.

What the hell was wrong with the name he'd been born under?

Edward Michaels had groomed Stavros to take over Dýnami Pharmaceutical, but on his terms. Stavros was sick of it. He had poured enough of his own blood and sweat into the company to have earned his place at the top, yet his grandfather kept pointing Stavros toward the bevy of potential brides in Manhattan, ordering him to select one if he wanted control of his birthright.

Stavros had been so resistant to the idea of marriage, he hadn't looked there or anywhere else.

Suddenly, however, he had a vision of Calli circulating through that social reef. Her thick black hair and elegant figure would look stunning in a burlap sack, let alone a designer gown. In fact, even without cosmetics or a high-end hairstyle, she would stand out as exotic against all those pale, blue-eyed blondes.

None of those overworked beauties possessed so much as a hint of warmth or passion, but when he had kissed Calli, she had matched his lust breath for breath. His blood ran hot as he recalled how responsive she was. Under the hand of a talented teacher, she would be incandescent.

That sort of passion would burn out, of course, but a marriage could be temporary, too.

It hadn't occurred to him to arrange both a marriage and a divorce when he'd been ordered by his grandfather to choose from their existing circle, but if she was a nanny from Greece with much lower expectations?

To hell with buying back his old house as a way of putting his grandfather on notice that his life was his own. There were better ways. *Greek immersion*, Stavros thought with wry delight. The kind that included sinking into a divine Hellenic figure every night and exchanging pillow talk in the language of his birth. He throbbed just imagining it, his skin growing tight, blood burning in his veins.

And when he considered the look on his grandfather's face as he presented a Greek wife…

A grim smile crept across his mouth.

Calli managed to sneak out of the house as Stavros was doing a final sweep of the courtyard. Takis had been quick to follow her outside all week, getting between them and not giving her a chance to have so much as a private word with Stavros, let alone private *time*.

Stavros hadn't made a concerted effort to see her, though, which had begun to erode her confidence. She was feeling bereft. Cast off, even.

It was silly. She and Stavros weren't even lovers! Not really.

"It's beautiful," she told him as she gazed in wonder at the transformed courtyard.

Whether he was a certified tradesman or not, he was meticulous and talented. He had managed to replicate the subtle pattern from the driveway, which was more complex than it looked on first glance. She had spied on him while he worked, absorbed by the way he carefully measured and cut each tile, turning it this way and that to get it exactly right.

Rather than replant the trees that had broken the old tiles, he'd suggested they order pots of fragrant wisteria that would eventually climb the walls and overhead trellis. He had hung strings of white lights and now, as dusk fell, the scattered pinpricks were like stars that were close enough to touch. Pure magic.

When she brought her attention back to him,

she saw he was taking in her creased shorts and scoop-neck T-shirt, which amplified her insecurity. She'd been telling herself they were on the same level, that Takis was a snob, but she was very much an island peasant while Stavros was... She wasn't sure. *More.*

Somehow she knew she was outgunned.

"I, um..." Her nerve almost failed her, but each night she relived the way he'd made her feel and every morning she waited, hoping today would be the day she felt that way again. He was like a potent drug that only needed to provide one rush of ecstasy and she was hooked. It shocked her how atavistic this need was. How undeniable.

Her voice scraped from the narrow space between foolish courage and profound self-doubt. "I was going to suggest coming with you when you leave today, so I can drive the Vespa home."

Here is my self-respect. I brought it out of the vault. Please don't drop it.

Takis had *not* been impressed when he realized she was loaning out the Vespa. She hated that she had slipped a notch in his estimation, but she refused to dwell on it. She wasn't a child this time. Takis was not her father.

She wasn't being foolish. She was being a woman. Human.

Offering to go home with a man. For sex.

And maybe some give and take of the comfort she sensed they both needed.

"Tempting." A muscle ticked in his jaw and his gaze held memory and smug ownership as he swept it over her. "But Ionnes is coming to pick up the last of the equipment." He handed her the key for the scooter. "I'm riding with him, then leaving."

"For?"

"New York."

Déjà vu all over again.

She couldn't help a flinch of yearning at what he might see there, in ignorance, not the least bit aware it was everything to her.

"Want to come?" he asked in a way that suggested he knew she did.

She swallowed, feeling obvious and predictable. Why had she let him see this stupid sexual crush? Why let him distract her from her goals at all? She shook her head.

"Someday." The need to go to New York had been in every beat of her pulse for the last six years, but leaving Ophelia had grown harder over time, not easier. She hadn't been able to justify abandoning the girl for a wild-goose chase.

But she had never managed to confirm anything solid from this side of the world. Her only choice was to go to New York without a proper lead, which meant she would need time once she got there. She would have to get a job and support herself while she hunted, which meant getting a green card. She had started the process, but it wasn't easy, not when she was qualified for next to nothing. She had put her name in with some nanny agencies, but hadn't heard anything.

It was daunting and added to the old fearful certainty that she wasn't meant to be part of her son's life.

She lifted her gaze to look Stavros in the eye. The impact was like an arrow to the chest, but she hung on to that pain to ground herself. Dating was a luxury she couldn't afford. She had to remember that.

"Safe travels."

"I'll be back." His sensual mouth lost its skew of humor as he heard her words for the final goodbye it was. "I'll see you again. Soon."

She snorted, having played the game of waiting and wondering before. No. She would not let herself be that stupid again. A familiar trickle of humiliation invaded her bloodstream. *Fool.* Maybe she was still childish and immature.

"Don't bother. It wasn't meant to be." She offered a weak smile. "Take care."

As she turned away, he caught at her arm. "You're going to see me again, Calli."

Better not. Heart ripped from its moorings, she shrugged off his touch.

"Goodbye, Stavros." She went into the house.

CHAPTER FOUR

EVERY YEAR TAKIS celebrated his birthday with a huge bash. It happened to fall on the same day as a local festival that included fireworks on the water. He invited friends from the mainland and colleagues from his auditing firm. While he sometimes had a date for other events, for this one he always asked Calli to hostess. He rented her a gown and she stood at his side between keeping an eye on the local girls she'd brought in to serve the food she had prepared over the last two weeks. Ophelia had elected to stay with her grandparents on the mainland this year, claiming the event was hideously boring.

It was. Most of the conversation centered on finance or which hot car had been purchased by whom at what bargain price. At least Calli had done this enough times she knew most of the players and could inquire after a child or ask about the retirement party for so-and-so.

Many remarked on how nice the tiling looked around the pool, now it had been refreshed.

"Spending a lot this year, aren't you? Boarding school, now this." One of Takis's fellow auditors used a sharp gaze to add up the changes.

The game among Takis's workmates was always how *little* they spent, so she wasn't surprised by his response.

"I wouldn't have bothered, but Ionnes said he could do it at cost."

Calli had forgotten that was how the work had been approved. She'd pressed for it to happen later in the summer, worried it wouldn't be completed in time for this party, but Ionnes had insisted this was his only opportunity.

Because Stavros had been on his working vacation?

She was trying not to think of that man, but frowned up at Takis, wondering if he also thought it strange in retrospect.

He was looking past her, but not with his relaxed, charming host expression. He was stone-faced. Affronted.

She glanced, saw a new arrival in a tuxedo,

then did a double-take as she recognized that the clean-shaven, gorgeous man was—

"Oh, my God!"

If the dry smile on Stavros's sexy lips hadn't given him away, the way her blood leaped in her arteries did. That was definitely Stavros. She didn't react like this to any man except him.

You're going to see me again.

She had refused to let herself even think it, let alone believe it.

"Excuse me," Takis muttered, and drew Calli toward Stavros, muttering, "Did you invite him?"

"No." Despite being as drawn as ever by Stavros's magnetism, she had an urge to bolt. Takis's arm across her back held her fast.

Another *zing* of electricity shot through her as her gaze locked with Stavros's.

"We meet again. As promised," he said, then lifted his gaze to her employer's. "Takis." It was a flat greeting. Arrogant and dismissive. Very nearly disdainful.

"What are you doing here?" Takis demanded.

She imagined he was taking note of the tuxedo. It was no rental. It was obviously made to fit Stavros's honed form to perfection. He looked like a secret agent in a spy film as he accepted a flute of champagne from a circulating tray and sipped.

"Men of my caliber are always invited." He reached into the pocket of his tuxedo and handed over a card.

"You run Dýnami Pharmaceuticals," Takis said with disbelief, handing her the card that proclaimed this to be Steve Michaels, president.

"I prefer my Greek name, Stavros Xenakis. Stav, if *you* like," he said directly to Calli.

Her heart took another leap while something slithery and wonderful curled deep in her belly under his regard. She had known he was more than he seemed. Now whatever shade he'd been standing under was gone and his full, glorious power was on display. He was both blinding and breath-stealing.

"Technically my grandfather, the director, has last say on our biggest decisions. But that will change very soon." His gaze stayed on Calli as though she was some kind of linchpin to that statement. "Let's discuss how you'll help me with that, shall we?"

Her heart ping-ponged in her chest. "*I could never—*"

"This can't be real. Get out of my house, whoever the hell you are."

Stavros lifted a gaze that was both weary and completely uncompromising. "You negotiated a generous offer with an agent this morning. This house is mine." The corner of his mouth twitched. "But I'll graciously allow you to continue your party."

"What?" A wave of shock slammed into Calli, leaving her drained of all sensation, barely staying on her feet. She pulled from Takis's hold to look up at him.

Around them, the music and conversation continued. The lights sparkled and water splashed as a handful of couples laughed in the pool. A few faces glanced in their direction, making her conscious that she should keep her voice down and her expression neutral, but she couldn't take it in.

Takis wasn't able to hide his flash of culpability. "I countered by doubling it. I didn't think it would be accepted. I was going to tell you later. I can send you to New York, Calli."

Hot tears of panic filled her throat. It was one

thing to want something with every fiber of your being, quite another to go after it. What if it didn't work out? What if she failed? What if she found her son and he wanted nothing to do with her? *She wasn't ready!*

"That won't be necessary." There was a possessive edge to Stavros's tone. "Calli will be coming to New York with me. As my wife."

"What?!" Calli didn't realize she'd been holding a champagne flute until it hit the tiles and smashed, leaving a wet stain spreading on the fancy new tiles Stavros had laid and now possessed. She swore under her breath and shot an abashed look around.

"Let's take this somewhere private." Stavros took her elbow. "Clean that up, would you?" he ordered one of the servers who came hurrying toward them.

Calli jolted under the impact of his light touch and wanted to pull away, but she'd already made enough of a scene. Takis was drilling holes into her with his gaze, and the weight of the crowd's attention made her even hotter with embarrassment.

Rather than tightening his grip when he felt

her stiffen, Stavros gentled his touch, so it became a caress that sent furls of disarming heat into her belly.

"I don't want to talk to you," she told him as he crowded close, urging her toward the house. "What are you even doing here? Why *were* you here, pretending to be a pool man, if you're actually some kind of drug tycoon?"

"Now, see? That sounds like you do want to talk. Come. All will be revealed."

She quickly moved ahead of him, folding her arms and trying to rub away the lingering sensation of his touch as she entered the den that served as a home office for Takis.

Stavros closed the door firmly behind them.

She swung around, her entire body prickling with fight or flight. "Explain, then."

He lifted one brow at her tone, but only shrugged.

"It was a bet." His attention shifted to assess the spare decor of his new workspace. "My friend has a sense of humor. He challenged a few of us to go two weeks without our credit cards, claiming we couldn't survive it. I did. Thanks to you."

He shifted his weight onto one leg and flexed his foot to indicate where he'd had stitches.

"Congratulations," she bit out, watching him move to the liquor cabinet and help himself to the ouzo. "Why do you want this house?"

He didn't answer until he had poured and brought the small glasses across to her. She remembered thinking he would make an excellent poker player and thought it again as she tried to read his shuttered expression.

"Yamas." He clinked his glass to hers before throwing back his drink. "This was my home as a child. When my father died, my grandfather moved us to New York and sold it. I want it back."

His father. She recalled his anguish that day on the peninsula and knew it was his father he was still searching for, lost in that unforgiving water. Shadows of that old grief moved behind the shuttered stare he offered her now.

Her heart began to tilt toward him, like a flower reaching out to the sun, but she gave it a quick yank back. She couldn't afford to soften toward him.

"Must be nice to simply write a check and

get what you want. You realize that means I'm shoved off without a job or a home? *Thanks*."

"Your *job* will be 'wife of a drug tycoon.' I'll admit that 'heir to a multinational pharmaceutical research and manufacturing conglomerate' is a mouthful, but let's try to find some middle ground. What do you say?"

"I say you're a dishonest person, *Steve*. And I'm not going to marry you. What on earth makes you think I would?"

Stavros lifted a scathing brow. "Shall I remind you what we left unfinished between us?"

A flood of heat washed over her. It was a mix of embarrassment and memory, pleasure and the pain of rejection. She set aside her untasted ouzo and folded her arms.

"Key word. You *left*," she stated flatly. "I've moved on."

Something hard and bright flashed in his gaze. "With whom?"

"Takis." She lifted her chin to deliver the outrageous lie.

"Nice try, but I already know you didn't marry him when you had the chance. He's a bit of a fool, asking when you were already living a fine life without putting out or getting pregnant in exchange for it."

She fell back a step. "What a horrible thing to say!"

He shrugged. "True, though. Isn't it?"

"No!" Takis had been kind to her in a thousand ways. She deserved none of it, but she had never felt anything toward him except gratitude and affection. "Well, it's true I didn't want to get pregnant. But I also said no because I didn't love him. Not the way a wife should love her husband anyway. Which is why I won't marry *you*."

"That's good news. The part where you don't love either of us." He poured a fresh ouzo for himself. "As is the fact you don't want children."

She hadn't said *that*. She just wanted to find the child she'd already had before she thought about having more. She swallowed the lump that came into her throat and shifted her stance. "Look, buy the house. I can't stop you. But why on earth would you suggest we marry?"

"My grandfather has been pressuring me to find a wife. He's holding off stepping down as director until I do. All the women I know would demand a real marriage. By that I mean years of my life. Children. Half of my assets if we divorce."

"You don't like children?" It suddenly became a pivotal sticking point in a conversation that was too outlandish to be happening, but she couldn't help jumping to a vision of finding her son and watching Stavros reject him. Her heart began to thud in painful tromps.

"I'm told I need an heir, but I'm in no hurry." He swirled the clear liquid in the bottom of his glass. "In fact, I plan to leave that up to my sisters, but I'm impatient to take the reins of the company. I need a wife to present to my grandfather. One who will act the part but leave on cue. Why do you want to move to New York?"

"How do you know that? Have you had me investigated?" She paled as she wondered what he'd found.

"I overheard you and Takis one day. Why? Do you have a deep dark secret you want to stay buried?" He narrowed his gaze. "Tell me now. I don't want a scandal popping up to smudge the family name."

She knew people whispered on the island that she'd had a teen pregnancy. They all thought the baby had died and Stavros might hear that same rumor if he sent someone to snoop, but he wouldn't find a headstone for the boy. Her father had refused to pay for one. Because her son wasn't *dead*.

He was somewhere in New York. At least, his father, Brandon Underwood, was in New York and he knew where the infant had been placed.

"I have a normal desire for privacy," she said, glossing over her alarm. "I don't like the idea you're prying." But it was starting to hit her that Stavros had the means to pry. That *she* would have the means.

With Stavros's name and social standing behind her, she would have the power to confront Brandon. The cache to meet him on a level playing field, face-to-face.

The thought made her dizzy.

"You live in New York? That's where you want to take me?" she confirmed, trying to keep from hoping. It was too big, too fast. Too *easy*.

"Manhattan, yes. Why do you want to go?"

She touched her neck where it felt as though her pulse would burst the skin. Takis had tried to help, taking her to a lawyer who had written a couple of letters on her behalf, but Brandon's family had been too rich and influential, exactly as her mother had warned her. There was a death certificate on file, so she'd been dismissed as everything from an opportunist to a loony. Brandon claimed to have no recollection of her. As far as he was concerned, their affair had never even happened, let alone the birth of a boy his family had *stolen*.

Paid for, they might argue, if they ever admitted he'd been conceived at all.

"It's just always been a dream of mine," she prevaricated, folding her arms again and feeling the spike of her fingernails into her upper arms. Could she do this? Pretend to be a society wife and confront an old lover to find her son?

"Surely you could have managed a holiday if you wanted one?" The deep timbre of Stavros's voice seemed to come through water, hollow and barely penetrating her swimming thoughts.

"I want to live there. I've started the paperwork, but..." She shook herself out of becoming too attached to this crazy idea. It would devastate her if it didn't pan out. "It would be a green-card marriage," she warned. "Is that the sort of scandal you'd like to avoid?"

"You won't be working. Even after we separate, I'll support you. My lawyers can handle all of that very easily."

Must. Be. Nice.

"I still don't understand why you would ask *me*." A lowly nanny maid with no skills. No worth to society beyond what Takis and his daughter had bestowed upon her.

"As I said. You'll agree to something temporary and not clean me out as you leave. There will be a prenup and a suitable settlement. That's *all*. You realize that's what you're agreeing to? Six months should be enough time to transition my grandfather out."

"You're really offering a marriage on paper so you can—"

"Oh, Calli," he cut in. "Don't be naive. We'll share a bed. *That's* why I'm choosing you."

A burst of excitement exploded in her, making her turn her face to try to hide her reaction. He must have guessed, or seen her blush. Knowing laughter scraped from his throat.

"You're assuming I would want that," she said in a thin voice.

"I'm quite certain you do."

"Your arrogance is a turn-off."

"So is your denial of the truth."

She swung a glare toward him, instantly anxious that she had caused his interest to wane. He was *such* a dangerous man.

He set down his glass and held up his hands, motioning her to come to him. "Let's seal the deal."

"I need time to think." She scowled at the carpet, blind to the pattern and only seeing a blur of blues and greens. "This is happening too fast."

"It *will* happen fast." He came toward her, clasping her upper arms before she could properly catch her breath. "It has to. But you'll be paid out by Christmas and free to do as you please. So will I."

Christmas. With her son…

She barely dared allow such a sweet dream to form.

"You want me to sleep with you for personal gain." She choked on the words as she said them.

"We're going to sleep together either way."

"Do you have a subscription for that level of confidence? Because I'd love to know where it comes from."

"Right here, *glykia mou*. In the way you respond to me." Stavros pulled her up against him and wiped her brain clean with the first touch of his mouth, sending a shock of pained excitement through her, like she'd slammed into a wall of lightning.

With a moan of angst, she tried to hold back her response, not wanting to be so easy for him. To prove to herself she could resist him. *This*. But her body betrayed her. Her arms couldn't resist climbing to twine around his neck so she could hang on as the rest of her wilted and softened.

He felt so good, his strong arms supporting her, his hands stroking her lower back in a way that made her scalp tingle. She found herself opening her mouth beneath his, hungrily returning his kiss and welcoming the intrusion of his tongue. Losing herself in the waves of pleasure that rolled with increasing intensity through her.

In a brutal move of forced deprivation, he set her back on her flat feet, wet mouth curled into a cruel smile of satisfaction. "Need more proof?"

He wasn't even breathing hard. Not like she was.

It was humiliating, but it was the education she needed. She hated him enough in that moment to feel no twinge of conscience over using him. Not if he was going to use her libido to manipulate her.

Her level of desire scared her, though. Hormones had led her into heaven and hell once before. The joy of a son, the grief of losing him, all because she'd wanted someone to kiss her and treat her like she was special.

"You don't love me," she said through lips that felt scorched and puffy. It was a needle of truth that she plunged into herself, before he could do it, as a vaccine. She was trying to undercut the way she reacted to him, form antibodies so he wouldn't leave her devastated in six months.

"No," he agreed blankly. "I don't."

The needle bent and she gave it a twist, snapping it off.

"Don't say it. You lied once. Don't do it again. Don't make promises you won't keep. Don't…" She looked at her hands where she tangled her fingers in agitation.

She wanted to say, *Don't hurt me*. Not because

she was afraid for her physical self, but as much as she had learned to protect her heart, it was still a very thin-shelled, fragile thing.

A firm hand cupped her jaw and forced her to look into his eyes. "Don't?"

She pulled free of his touch before she melted and betrayed herself again. "This is a business agreement. Don't try to get inside my head."

He held her gaze and she tremored inside, wondering how anyone worked with a man this intense and powerful without incinerating under his laser regard.

"And I'm not sleeping with you until we're married."

A muscle in his cheek ticked. "Let's make it happen quickly, then."

Stavros had no best man. Alejandro was away on his challenge and Sebastien was witnessing Antonio's nuptials in Rome.

Antonio took the opportunity to provide sober second thoughts anyway, cautioning Stavros against taking a wife to appease his grandfather. "The first time I married, it was purely to serve family expectations. It was a disaster. Think twice, *amico*."

Stavros wasn't about to be swayed. "You're marrying for love this time, are you?" he challenged.

"I have a son." It was a face call and Stavros saw Antonio's jaw harden. His friend said nothing about the mother, Sadie.

Stavros had to wonder how a marriage like that could succeed, given the woman had kept such an explosive secret for so long, but he only said, "I want custody of my company. Same thing. And we've agreed it's only for six months."

"She said yes to that?" Antonio's brows lifted in surprise, then he shrugged as if to say, "Do what you like, then."

Stavros always did.

He ended the call, but soon heard from Alejandro. He thought he was about to get another warning, but aside from surprise, Alejandro passed no opinion on Stavros's marriage. He was more concerned with getting a DNA test for a horse.

What the hell was his friend facing in Kentucky?

Stavros had to wonder if Sebastien would think

this challenge was worth the loss of half his fortune. It *had* turned out more mentally taxing than Stavros had expected, but it had only increased his desire to take control of his own fortune, not to seek a higher purpose with his life.

His desire to claim Dýnami was the only reason, he told himself the next day, that his heart fishtailed in his chest when Takis arrived at the *dimarchio* alone.

The mayor had gone into his chamber moments ago and was waiting for them.

"Where's Calli?" he asked Takis.

"Ladies' room. She's not usually concerned about fussing with hair and makeup, but…" He glanced at his watch, then his gaze came up, level and unflinching. "You realize that if you hurt her, I'll kill you."

Possessiveness seared through Stavros's veins like a hit of heroin. His knee-jerk reaction was to come down like a hammer on the man, but in the few dealings he'd had with Takis, he'd found him to be direct and genuinely interested in Calli's welfare. Stavros had to respect him for that.

So he only said, "My prospects are considerably better than a pool boy's. She'll be well taken care of."

"She was already well taken care of."

"If that was all she wanted, she would have married you when she had the chance." It was a bit of a low blow, but Stavros was fishing. He knew Calli was getting something more from their marriage than a trip to New York and a generous settlement. He wanted to know what it was. The answer might lie in her reason for refusing Takis. What had her employer failed to provide for her?

Takis had the grace to darken beneath his swarthy complexion.

"I knew she was too young for me." His voice sharpened to defensive. "But I was running out of time to provide Ophelia with a brother or sister, and I knew what people were saying about Calli's presence in my house. They both deserved better."

His mouth grew so tight, a white line appeared around his lips.

"Regardless how she reacted to my proposal, I have to respect her decision to accept yours. Even if I have my reservations." His baleful glance was another warning. "She knows she has a home with us if it doesn't work out. Don't send her back to me in pieces."

Again Stavros told himself this catch of aggression was only because Calli leaving their marriage early could threaten his plan to take control of Dýnami, but there was more. There was something about the connection between her and this man that kicked him in the gut.

The sound of two pairs of high-heeled shoes approached and he lifted his gaze, then caught his breath as the image of his bride slammed into him.

The dress was simple, but Greek goddess–like in style. The front came down in a sharp V, hugging her breasts in gathered cups right above a wide band that emphasized her waist. Below it, the white silk draped gracefully to just past her knees. A handful of tiny white flowers had been woven into her hair and she held a bouquet of pink roses.

Her hand went to her middle as she saw him. "It's overkill, isn't it? I told you," she said to Takis, wincing self-consciously.

"No," Stavros insisted, shrugging on the suit

jacket he had removed outside because of the heat. "You look beautiful." He held out his arm.

"I told you it was perfect." Ophelia wore pastel pink. She was coltish and pretty, not unlike Calli in her quintessential Greek looks, and glowed with importance as she took her father's arm and followed them into the mayor's office.

Minutes later, Stavros kissed his wife with a thrill of triumph. Strangely, the prize he most anticipated claiming was not the corporation. He was suddenly annoyed with himself that he had only booked a few short days—and nights—in Paris before he took Calli to New York.

It was an odd shift in priorities that he put down to sexual frustration, but these few days of making arrangements had been interminable. The last thing he had patience for was a drawn-out goodbye between Calli and her employer, especially when it put tears in her eyes.

"Thank you," she choked as she hugged Takis. "I'm sorry."

"For what? You silly girl." Takis rubbed her upper arms. "I'm the one who is sorry. I know I let you down. If I hadn't, you wouldn't be doing this."

"No! You gave me so much. Now I'm leaving like I don't appreciate it, but I do. I swear I do."

"All I ever gave you was a chance. You earned everything else. I wish you luck." His face grew grave and concerned. "Call me. Any time, for any reason. Understand?"

She nodded.

"I mean it."

"I know," she murmured and turned to his daughter. Ophelia sobbed openly and they hugged a long time, Calli murmuring reassuring noises to the teenager. "*You* call *me* anytime," she said as they finally broke apart. "For any reason."

"I love you, Calli."

"I love you, too. Stay out of trouble, *paidi mou.*" There was such conflict, such an agony of torn loyalty in Calli's expression, Stavros felt guilty taking her hand and drawing her away, like he was wrenching her from her family.

If she felt so close to them, why was she marrying him?

He wanted to believe the answer was obvious. Money, of course, but she had seemed rather ambivalent about the settlement they had negotiated, saying only, "Wow. You really want this marriage. I'll try to live up to that."

She hadn't tried to negotiate the value higher so he had wound up increasing the ceiling amount himself. He hadn't lied to Takis when he had said she would be well taken care of, even if she didn't know how to do that herself.

He was still thinking about that, wondering about her reasons for wanting this marriage, when they were settled aboard his private jet. He watched her turn his rings round and round on her finger as though having second thoughts.

"What else did Takis give you besides a job?" he asked.

Her brows came together in dismay as she turned her head to look at him. After a surprised pause, she settled her hands in her lap and said, "I thought we agreed to keep this just business."

"We have to talk about something for the next six months. You didn't like the idea of my investigating you. Tell me yourself what you want me to know."

Her chin set and she rearranged the fall of her skirt. She was still in her wedding dress, but it didn't seem out of place. It seemed rather apropos, given the virginal nerves emanating off her.

In the back of his mind, he kept thinking of that overheard conversation, when Takis had said, *What happened to waiting until you're married? She wasn't a virgin, was she? In this day and age?*

"He gave me a home. Trust. Respect." He heard poignancy in her tone, like she feared she had lost those things all over again.

Stavros trusted her. To a point. He respected her as much as he respected any form of life. Maybe a little more, since she had the capacity for kindness and humor. Nevertheless, he was fairly sure his money was not her goal. She had other motives he had yet to determine. That produced a natural caution in him.

"He said he asked you to marry him because people were gossiping about your arrangement."

"They were. But I had already put up with it for two years. I didn't see the point in trying to change it just because I had turned nineteen. Frankly, they still would have talked. The age difference was that wide. And I didn't think of him that way."

He hadn't realized how young she was until he

had filed for the marriage license. She didn't look more than the twenty-three she was, but there was a maturity in her demeanor that suggested she was a lot older.

"You were seventeen when you went to live with him?" Maybe she was a virgin. "Where were your parents?"

"They live on the island." Something in her tone warned him he was treading dangerous ground.

He had asked if her parents would be coming to Athens for the wedding. Her flat no had half convinced him they were dead.

"Did they disapprove of your living with Takis?"

"They disapproved of a lot of things."

He suspected that was a colossal understatement, given the marble-like smoothness of her profile. "Is that *why* you moved in with Takis? Did you run away?"

"They kicked me out." Her hands clenched into fists, crushing the delicate silk of her dress. "I was sleeping on the beach. It's a small island. Everyone knew my business. I thought it would be better to get to the mainland, but I didn't have ferry fare. Takis was the richest man on the island. I knew he was widowed. When I saw him waiting in his car for the ferry…"

Her mouth pursed. Bright red flags of shame rose in her cheeks as she turned her head to look at him, but she met his gaze without quailing. Defiant almost, while the shadows of anguish in her eyes made the honey gold of her irises hard as amber.

A spike of nausea went into his gut, anticipating what was coming, even though he somehow wanted to travel back in time and prevent the exchange she was about to admit to.

"I made him an offer he kindly refused." She tried to smooth the creases from her skirt as she realized how badly she had wrinkled it. "He knew there are plenty of men in this world who wouldn't hesitate to take advantage of a desperate teenager, though. He was on his way to pick up Ophelia from her grandparents and hire a new nanny. She was running through them like penny candy. He said he would give me a shot, but made it clear he wouldn't tolerate drugs or stealing or anything else like that. He's not a bleeding heart."

"Is that why your parents threw you out? Drugs? Stealing?"

"No." It took her a minute to continue. Her hands twined together so tightly her nail beds turned white. "I, um, messed around with a tourist. My father said I shamed him."

Ah. Not a virgin. He was disappointed, but not for possessive reasons. He sensed that experience had colored her view of men and sex.

"Is that why you wanted to wait until marriage to sleep with me? Because you had premarital sex and got thrown out for it?"

She hitched a shoulder. She was back to offering only her profile, and blinked rapidly. "I just didn't want to be used again. At least this time it's mutual." Her mouth quirked with distaste. "I won't be left with nothing."

That mercenary streak of hers shouldn't have chafed. He ought to find it comforting, he supposed, since it made her motives seem really straightforward, but he found himself saying, "I wondered why you were leaving him when you're obviously very attached. Money does make the girl turn round, doesn't it?"

She swiveled just her head, eyes wide with hurt

and something else. Bitter astonishment. "Are you pointing out that I haven't risen very far from offering myself to Takis for ferry fare? I'm aware. But you married for money, too. If you find my behavior distasteful, it's because you're looking in a mirror."

Calli had already been reeling over what she'd done before Stavros had pushed a stiletto of an insult between her ribs.

She judged herself harshly enough, thanks. She'd married a stranger so he would take her to America. She was going to sleep with him and pose as his wife so she could search for her son.

Takis had nearly come apart at the seams when she had told him what she had agreed to. Ophelia's mother had been the love of Takis's life, but he cared for Calli. Under his blunt exterior, he had always been protective of her, which was sweet, but as time wore on, it had also begun to abrade. Ophelia had said her father smothered and controlled. It was his way of trying to prevent the people he cared about from being hurt, but even with the search for Calli's son, Takis had always been too quick to take the lead and make a call and act as go-between.

She had felt held back, but she had let him shield her for a number of reasons, not least of which was her belief, deep down, that she was to blame for what had happened. She feared she wasn't good enough to be a part of her son's life. Brandon's family hadn't thought so. Her own parents had berated her for going through with the pregnancy then orchestrated Dorian's removal from her custody. She had failed to hang on to him, had failed to even find out where he was.

She had failed as a mother.

So what right did she have to search for Dorian now? Would he even want anything to do with her? He was so young. Six. Was he in school? He might not even know he was adopted.

Was he adopted? Loved?

Takis had assured her more than once that powerful families didn't like surprises from the past cropping up. They controlled them from the outset, which was why they had taken their grandson and cut his humbly born mother out of the picture as ruthlessly as possible. People at their level didn't let their heir apparent marry an island girl knocked up during a holiday romance. They paid her off, then ensured their son's slip-up was given a silver spoon and an Ivy League education.

Takis was convinced Dorian was in a good situation. Brandon's family wouldn't have taken him if they only wanted to put him in foster care and forget about him. They could have left him in Greece if being raised by strangers had satisfied them.

But was he loved?

That was Calli's best wish for Dorian, but there was a dark side to that shiny coin. If he was happy, then having his birth mother arrive to disrupt things could be traumatic for him.

Until she knew exactly what kind of situation he was in, however, until she knew he *was* safe and loved, she would never rest easy. She would always be tortured by this sense that she had let him down.

"You don't like it?"

Stavros's voice startled her out of her introspection. "Pardon?"

"He's one of the top chefs in Paris, but you

don't seem pleased. Shall I call back the staff and request something else?"

They'd been speaking to each other in stilted phrases since she had swiped back at him on the plane. Now she looked at the meal she had rearranged on her plate, but barely tasted.

"It's fine. Excellent. I'm just…distracted. I'm, um, sorry I was so bitchy on the plane. This is a big step I've taken. It's finally hitting me."

His brows twitched with surprise at her apology. His cheeks went hollow, then he made a dismissive gesture. "Your remark struck too close to home. And, to be quite honest, my time fixing the pool tiles allowed me to see what a nuisance it is to lack money."

"A 'nuisance,'" she repeated drily. "Do tell."

He shrugged off her sarcasm. "Even then, I had friends at the end of a telephone line and knew my dire straits were only for two weeks. I wasn't sleeping on a beach. When I think of you as a young girl in that situation…"

His sharp gaze was hard to bear.

She hated thinking about that time, too.

She sipped the very excellent white wine that had been paired with their meal for this private dining experience in a honeymoon suite with a view of the Eiffel Tower, then tried to lighten the mood.

"The beach was nothing. I've spent the last six years with a girl going through puberty. Forget two weeks without credit cards. I challenge you to survive *that*."

He chuckled into his own glass as he took it up. "Pass."

"That's what I thought." She took a bite and chewed slowly, awash in the conflict of leaving Ophelia. She didn't know about Dorian. Takis had left it to Calli to tell her if the timing ever felt right. It was such a very difficult subject. Calli had only ever opened up about it with Takis. Now she wondered if she should have explained better to Ophelia why she was marrying and moving to New York.

"You'll miss her," Stavros said.

"I will. When I first came to live with them, she was a nightmare. Did horrible things. Poured sand in my bed. Played dead in the pool. Got into Takis's liquor cabinet. The first sip made her cough and I heard her, so not much damage there, but still." Calli shuddered to remember those first months.

"She resented anyone in the house who wasn't her mother and wanted her father to stay home with her, but he couldn't. I was quite open about the fact I had nowhere else to go. I told her it didn't matter what she did, we were stuck with each other. Then one day we saw my mother as we were running errands."

Calli's appetite dried up again and she set aside her cutlery.

"Ophelia realized there could be something more awful than your mother dying. She could be alive and refuse to look at you." The agony of that painful moment caused a flinch she couldn't control, tightening her voice even though she attempted to sound unaffected.

Things had never changed and Calli doubted they ever would. Her mother had had opportunities to back her up about Dorian being taken, when Takis had first tried to help, but she had stuck with the story that the baby had died. She had aligned with Calli's father and Calli would never forgive either of them.

"Ophelia still pulled pranks after that, but they

weren't so malicious. We started having fun together."

They had grown so close that by the time Calli first scraped together enough of her wages for airfare to New York, but *just* airfare, she had been reluctant to abandon Ophelia. She was finally settling down. Her grades had improved and Takis wasn't as worried as he'd been.

Calli had let Takis talk her into staying a little longer, unwilling at that point to confess to him her reasons for wanting to leave. It had been too humiliating, and it had felt good to hear how much she was needed by him and Ophelia. For the first time in her life, she had felt valued. Loved.

"She's excited to go away to school, but I know she's anxious, too. Now you've bought her home and I'm leaving for New York. It's a lot for her. I feel guilty." Torn.

"Regretful?"

"No." She was able to state that in a quiet, but firm tone of resolve. Whatever happened in New York would be painful. That was a given, but this was too much of a golden opportunity to get answers. She couldn't let anything hold her back.

Not this time. "No, I'm quite committed to going through with this."

"I'll try to make it pleasant enough you don't have to simply endure it," he drawled.

"What? Oh, that did sound awful, didn't it?" She blushed and covered her hot cheeks. "I didn't mean it like that!"

"I know." His voice held humor, but confidence and anticipation, too.

It provoked a ripple of awareness, sending restlessness prickling through her. She had been avoiding thinking about sex. It had been a kind of denial as she focused only on what she would get with this marriage, not on what she would give up.

Or how easily he made her give up *so much*.

"Has there been anyone since that tourist?"

"No." She was struck with performance anxiety as she admitted it.

"Why would you do that to yourself when you're so sensual?"

"It was my first time. It was clumsy and awkward, not something I was excited to try again. Why do you feel a need to make conquests of women when you're barely interested in them?"

He snorted. "You do love to go on the attack when you feel threatened, don't you?" He threw his napkin onto his plate and rose. "Quit being so nervous. I was serious about making it good for you. And now I know how inexperienced you are, I'll take it slow." He drew her to her feet and into a close dance.

She stiffened, but couldn't, simply couldn't remain tense when everything in her was drawn to melt and soften against him. His touch made her shiver, especially when he found the low back of her dress and traced the edge, leaving a tickling line of fire against her skin.

With a wince that she hid with a duck of her head, she let herself succumb to his hold until she was resting against him.

"I have not stopped thinking about the way you moved against me that day, *koukla mou*." His voice was a low rumble in his chest. "How you ignited and made those erotic noises as you hit your peak."

"Don't remind me. It's embarrassing."

"It's arousing. Does it not turn you on to remember?"

It did. She was growing weak, even though

they were talking about something that made her squirm. His body brushed against hers. They moved in a slow rock that didn't even match the muted instrumental music playing in the background. Was he hard? Was that what she had just felt as her stomach grazed his pelvis? All of her senses came alive to him. Attuned. All of her cells honed in like magnets attracted to the polarity in his. She held her breath, waiting for the next brush of contact.

"You don't want to hear that I relive it every night? That I can't sleep unless I let myself imagine I took you against that wall until we were both groaning and shuddering in a shared release?" His lips nuzzled her neck, making her whimper.

"Don't be graphic."

"Sex is graphic. You and I will have a lot of sex, *glykia mou.* Get used to the idea. Nerves are fine, but I can see you trying to resist what you feel and I don't like it. You're the one who said you don't want lies between us."

She stopped moving and glared up at him. "You really think you own me and the entire world, don't you?"

He lifted a hand to smooth back her loose hair, then slowly closed his fist into the mass at the back, not hurting, but holding her still as he lightly teased his mouth against hers, making her lips burn.

"You and your world. For the next six months. Beg me to kiss you."

"No."

He released a breath of hot laughter against her chin and lowered to almost but not quite kiss the side of her neck.

She tried to wriggle free, but his grip was implacable. He only lifted his head, leaving the skin at her nape tingling in anticipation, yet aching with loss. Everything in her wanted to beg him for that kiss, but she set her chin, refusing to.

"If you want me to stop, say so, but if it's yourself you're fighting then tell me why. Is it because you were raised to think it's wrong to like sex?"

"I don't have hang-ups, if that's what you're asking. I just don't like feeling manipulated by someone who treats my body like it's territory on a game board. You're not sensual at all. You're more turned on by the idea of conquering me."

His expression hardened and a bright light

filled his eyes. "The only reason I didn't take you against the wall that day was because I didn't have a condom. Stop fighting how much you want me and I'll show you how much I want you," he promised.

Or was it a threat?

Either way, it was a huge risk. Scary. She didn't have a hang-up about sex, not really, but she didn't like letting her basest self overcome her rational brain. Biology was a powerful thing, designed by nature to perpetuate the species no matter the cost to the parents. The way Brandon had made her feel had been a tepid bath compared to the way she reacted to Stavros, but she had still allowed that bit of pleasantness to override her good sense.

The result had been a disaster, and she was terrified her life would spin out of control again, especially when the temptation to allow it was so strong.

"I won't beg, either," he said in a gravelly undertone, drawing a tendril of her hair across the base of her neck. "Even though I want you more than… I keep thinking it's because of the way we met. *Where* we met."

His gaze was fixated on the silk of her hair drawn across her skin, his voice a rasp.

"Don't imagine I could walk out of here and enjoy the next woman who comes along. I want *you*," he said.

She couldn't help the cut of her breath against the pressure on her throat. Her pulse leaped at the same time, while a flood of heat washed through her.

"I—" She tried to swallow. "I started a prescription, but it's not working yet. You have to wear something until it is. I don't want to get pregnant."

It was a desperate attempt to slow things down, not that it had any effect on either of them.

"I won't forget."

They held a locked stare for a minute, something that was between a power struggle and a quest for reassurance. On her part, at least. She didn't know what it was for him. She didn't know *him*, which was distressing. But she looked into his eyes and sensed… Maybe she was projecting what she wanted to see, but she sensed that she could be his salvation in a way that she wanted him to be hers.

That reflection of herself in there, that sense that he wrestled in his own cage of agony, got to her every time.

Her gaze dropped to his mouth.

As if it was the signal he'd been waiting for, he set one brief, openmouthed kiss on her lips. A test. Was she ready for this? Would she respond as he'd asked?

She was. She did. Only this time she didn't just let her lips cling to his. When he came back for a longer kiss, she kissed him back. She didn't just let the wash of pleasure guide her reaction, she responded with intention. Encouragement. She revealed the hunger that had been prowling inside her from the first moment she had seen him.

A growl sounded in his throat as he took control of the kiss, deepening it.

She moaned, let him have his way, but splayed her fingers in his hair and massaged. His arms tightened, drawing her already hot body tight against the inferno that was his, making her breathless.

With each tiny reaction, the intensity pinballed tighter and faster between them. She arched into him; he gave her his tongue. She met the intrusion with a delicate suction and he made a ragged noise while moving wide, possessive hands over her back and hips. Her waist. When she rocked her breasts against his chest, both trying to ease the ache in the tips and incite his reaction, he caught one in his splayed fingers.

The sensation had her opening her eyes, but she saw nothing, all of her vision white. A flood of wet heat poured into the juncture of her thighs while he plucked and rolled her nipple through her dress and bra. A plea caught in her throat, begging him to strip her so she could feel that hot, sensual touch on her bare skin. *Please.* She thrust her pelvis into his.

He pivoted and stumbled her backward. They bumped an end table. A lamp hit the floor with a clattering smash, jolting her back to their elegant surroundings.

"What—"

"Forget it," he ordered, fingers working behind her. "Where is the zip?"

"It's here—" She lifted her arm, panting, but as her hand came up she couldn't resist cupping his jaw and chasing his mouth with her own.

He avoided her long enough to say, "Give me

your tongue," then he kissed her, made a feral noise as she gave herself up to him and got her dress open enough to sweep his fingertips across the lace of her bra.

They fell to the sofa, angled and crooked, each with one leg hanging off. His knee dug into the cushion beside her hip and they both writhed a moment until he pulled back and guided her inside knee so he was between her legs. The skirt of her dress fell to her waist, baring her lacy white panties.

He took a moment to look from the scrap covering her hips to where her dress gaped at her shoulder. His carved features were more savage than ever. She shouldn't find it a turn-on, but her wetness increased. She shakily pulled her shoulder from her dress, then opened her bra, baring her breast.

She offered herself in the most blatantly scary way. *Please like what you see.*

His lips tightened across his teeth in something too feral to be a smile, then he covered her and took her nipple into his mouth, hot and assertive, sucking strongly so she bucked against him.

"Stavros!"

"Too much?" He drew back to circle with his tongue and scrape lightly with his teeth. "Or not enough? Tell me," he ordered in a guttural tone.

All she could say was a whispered *"More"* while she scored her nails across his shoulders, wishing she could tear open his shirt and feel his skin.

He kept teasing her while he lifted his chest enough to yank at his buttons, tearing open his shirt then making a noise of satisfaction as she slid her hands beneath it, stroking hot, flexing muscle, squirming with pleasure at the way he dallied at her breast and pulled at her other shoulder until both her breasts were available to him.

She was being utterly wanton, shocking herself, but the way he pulled back in a kind of sexual daze was incredibly exciting. How could she not thrill to the power in arching her back and hearing his breath grow ragged?

"Not scared now, are you? You should be," he said in a dangerous voice, stroking a hand up her inner thigh and catching at the damp fabric of her undies. His fingers went under and the backs of his knuckles grazed the seam of her lips, making her stomach muscles tense and jump.

He grunted approval. "Like that?"

She was trembling all over, unable to speak, to say she *loved* it. She moved one fingertip to his fly, tracing the ridge that pressed at the front.

He bit out a curse and, with a jerk of lace, he bared her to his avid gaze.

She squeaked in surprise, then caught her breath as he jerked open his fly with an equal lack of finesse and revealed himself.

Oh. That was… They were really doing this. He rolled a condom down his length, stroked himself with his fist as though ensuring a tight fit.

Her thighs twitched and she felt too exposed, too vulnerable. It was all happening so fast. Her hands went to his chest as he started to cover her.

His gaze flashed as he saw the hesitation in her eyes. "Say yes. Say yes, *please.*"

She wasn't sure if he was ordering her to beg or pleading for her to give him permission. The hint of desperation in his expression reassured her, though. He looked like he thought he might die if they didn't do this. It was enough to convince her he was as engulfed in this experience as she was.

With a tentative touch, she slid her hand between them and guided him into place. Like it was a signal, he took control again, covering her mouth in a passionate kiss as he pressed into her.

There was a pinch and a stretch, but "Mmm…" She groaned in joy, stunned by the rush of sensation as he moved in a testing stroke. He trembled and lifted enough to look at her, his gaze intense, as though holding back took all his effort.

Nothing in her life had ever felt this good and she wanted more. Needed it. Demanded it. She arched, inviting a deeper penetration on his next return.

His breath rasped and he drove a little harder and drew back to do it again. From there they abandoned any attempt at propriety and gave themselves up to the wildness of it. It was primitive and raw. Graphic. But good. So sinfully good.

She heard herself urging, "Never stop. Never."

"Never," he growled, driving her higher with every powerful move of his hips. They clung and arched and moaned and, when the crisis arrived released jagged cries as they crested together.

CHAPTER FIVE

STAVROS LANDED ON his back on the floor when he rolled off her, knocking out what little breath he had left. His elbow bumped the coffee table when he eventually lifted his wrist from his eyes.

All he could see was one bare knee off the edge of the sofa cushion and a flash of torn white lace abandoned on the glass of the tabletop.

He licked lips that were dry from panting. His breath and pulse slowed, but remained unsteady. He swallowed and rubbed his hand down his face, trying to pull himself together.

What the hell had just happened? He had promised to take it slow.

He had known it would be good and had wanted to savor their first time, but damn. They were a seriously combustible combination. The part of himself that carried a million responsibilities, and remained in control while taking on crazy physical stunts, told him to step back and reassess.

The other part, the part that went hang-gliding and ran with the bulls merely to keep from dying of boredom, that man was beating his chest and screaming a primal "Hell, yeah" from a mountaintop.

Her leg twitched and she made a noise. Discomfort?

Concerned, he forced his lethargic muscles to work and rose on one arm. The rest of him came back to life as he came eye level with her landscape of curves *en déshabillés*.

"Are you okay?"

"Fine." She pushed her skirt down and tried to draw up her rumpled dress to cover her breasts.

He hitched his elbow on the side of the sofa, set his chin on his fist and patiently waited for her gaze to quit skittering in avoidance. She finally turned her head so mere inches separated her nose from his. Such adorable shyness after they'd been rapacious and lost to one another. Did she remember demanding *more* from him? Telling him to never stop?

He would never forget it.

His scalp tightened all over again.

"Do you think we could make it to the bed this

time?" His voice came out more tender than he intended.

Her eyes widened. "You want to…again?" She swallowed.

He reminded himself she was the next thing to a virgin. "I did warn you we'd be doing it a lot." Say yes. *Please.*

Her pretty mouth drew into a moue and her lashes swept down. If she was physically uncomfortable, he would accept it, but if she was about to trot out one of her fibs about not wanting him, he would press harder. Surely they were past that now?

Surely she wanted to slake this voracious animal as much as he did?

"Perhaps if you gave me a head start?" She cut a dry glance toward him.

"Ha!" A rush of delight had him grabbing her and dragging her down atop him, laughing openly when she squealed in surprise. He caught at her dress, sweeping it upward and off as she wriggled to sit up across his hips.

They both stilled as he took in her naked figure.

She brought up a shy arm and he stopped her before she could cover herself. She blushed and bit her lip as she peered at him from behind hair that was loose and messy, framing her flushed face. Her curves were ample and soft, pale where she had protected herself from the sun. Mesmerizing.

He was humbled in that moment by her innocent beauty. By the feminine grace of her.

As he absorbed that this sensual, glorious woman belonged to him, it struck him that if he had grown up on their island, he might have been the one to take her virginity. Would he have married her? Had a lifetime with her?

It was a disturbing thought, like believing in fate, but it just went to show that the mistake he had made that day with his father continued to have repercussions.

He felt like a thief then, like he was stealing something he wasn't supposed to have.

He had long ago learned to live in the moment, however, not pine for what had been or what could be. He and Calli had an agreement. They had six months.

He would enjoy every one of them.

If it was possible to be punch-drunk from lovemaking, Calli was exactly that by the time they arrived in New York. They had even made love on the plane, since Stavros had a private jet with a stateroom.

When Calli thought back to her awkward fumblings with Brandon, something she'd done to feel close to a boy who had dazzled her, there was no comparison. It was the same act in name only.

Stavros took pains to make her soar, almost like it was a contest. Like every single time he was proving to her that he could make her feel like that. He seemed to take incredible pleasure in it, which was addictive in another way. She feared she was becoming infatuated, because how could she not fall for a man who provided such intense gratification with such delight in such an intimate way?

At the same time, the feeling that she was bought and paid for grew. When they had taken a break from lovemaking, their honeymoon had consisted of a lot of shopping. Obscenely decadent amounts of shopping.

She had protested, claiming the dresses, shoes and jewelry weren't necessary, but he had insisted. *We'll have a lot of appearances. You'll need to look the part.*

She wasn't his real wife. He wasn't spoiling her

because he wanted to. He was paying her to be something he needed.

The number of parcels that had been loaded onto the plane had made her feel uncomfortable, especially when he had called for a particular bag from a lingerie boutique to be brought into the cabin.

I want to see you in the red set.

Try as she might to feel objectified by that, when he had skimmed his lips along the lace at her hips, drawing it down oh-so-slowly, she had begged for the pleasure of his tongue. Twice.

She was losing herself. It was especially disturbing because, despite the intensity of time they were spending together and the physical familiarity they had arrived at, she still felt as though he was a stranger. Especially once he dressed in a tailored suit on the plane and began firing orders at everyone from his driver to the people he spoke with on the phone as they drove into Manhattan.

Somehow she had failed to fully appreciate how rich and powerful Stavros was. Yes, he had bought her countless gowns and dresses from boutiques and salons in Paris, but she hadn't seen any price tags. She had told herself they couldn't be that expensive.

She knew they were. She read gossip magazines. She knew designer dresses could make mortgage payments for average people like her. One bra alone had been her weekly salary. Stavros had bought it in every color.

She was in a state of denial because she couldn't believe she was awake, not dreaming this ridiculous charade she had put herself in.

When they arrived at a freestanding mansion in the middle of the city, however, she began to fully take in what kind of family she had married into. What kind of *money*. The bricks of the three-story house were a mellowed, burnt orange in the fading sun of the summer evening. The white detailing gave it an elegant Mediterranean feel. It had a proper stone balustrade surrounding a private garden and a wrought iron gate that didn't make a sound as Stavros held it open for her, allowing her to precede him up the stone path lined with fragrant lavender and thyme.

"This is your home?"

"My grandfather's town house. He stays here three nights a week and spends the rest of the week upstate. I did the same until I had access to my trust and bought my penthouse."

"You have a penthouse? In New York?"

"I have several." He shrugged it off as no big deal. "Simpson." Stavros greeted the man who opened the front door before they finished climbing the steps.

"Master Michaels. Welcome." He greeted Calli with a nod and showed them down the hall. He knocked briefly, then entered a den, announcing, "Your grandson, sir."

The elderly man leaned forward to press a button that muted the television, not rising until he saw Stavros had company. He was heavyset with age, but moved spryly and had an old-world stateliness to his handsome features. The Xenakis genes aged well. Stavros would grow more good-looking over time, as if he needed any more advantages.

"Will you be dining with us, sir?" Simpson asked.

"No, we'll have a proper family dinner later in the week, with my mother and sisters. This is a courtesy visit. To introduce my wife. Edward Michaels, Calli Xenakis."

The old man straightened another inch, plainly astonished.

The rest of what Stavros said should have been directed at the butler, but Stavros's hard stare remained locked with his grandfather's.

"You'll refer to both of us by our Greek names from now on."

If Calli had landed in a state of denial, she was nursing white-hot anger by the time she stood in the lounge of one of Stavros's many penthouses. Uniformed staff finished unloading her parcels from a dolly, hurrying to finish before tugging their caps as they left.

She dragged her gaze off the open-plan main floor with its ultramodern furniture in masculine tones of charcoal and silver. The stairs climbed at different angles to multiple levels, pausing on a landing where a small sitting room provided a space to enjoy the expansive view over the city through the massive wall of windows. The uppermost flight of stairs ended in a loft she presumed was the bedroom.

"Don't worry about unpacking. People will be here tomorrow."

"People. More bodies you've purchased for use?" She stared with contempt at the mountain of parcels piled up like stacks of money against the wall. Another rich playboy who did as he pleased. She had pegged him right from the first, but had still fallen for his line. She really was the stupidest woman alive.

"Explain that remark." His tone might have scared her if she wasn't so appalled. And hurt. Profoundly hurt.

"You picked me specifically to annoy your grandfather!"

Greece? That's where you've been?

She had seen the disapproval in the old man's eyes. The flinch as Stavros revealed she had been born on "his" island, like he knew it would get at the old man as nothing else could. The way Edward had stood there, silent and baleful as some kind of silent war raged between them, had stung like a snakebite.

"I *paid* you to annoy him." He waved at the parcels. "And I've included a tip."

"Why would I wear any of that when the point is to embarrass him? To *be* an embarrassment." Humiliation choked off her voice, burning hotly behind her eyes. "That's an ugly thing to do to someone. I'm not going to be part of it."

She moved to stab the button that called the private elevator.

"We have an agreement." He pushed a button labeled Cancel, then leaned on the wall next to it, blocking her from hitting the call button again. "A legally binding contract."

"That's what happens when you shop the bargain basement, *Steve*. You don't get the longevity you expect from the item. Move." She jerked her chin, wanting to punch right through him to the button he was blocking.

"Don't call me that," Stavros growled, prickling with what might have been his conscience.

"Don't call you Steve? It's better than what I want to call you. I'd take it, if I were you. *Move*." She dodged behind him, but he only flattened his back on the panel, aware he was being juvenile, but he hadn't expected this.

"You're overreacting."

"I'm reacting with the exact amount of outrage that is appropriate. You lied to me. You are exactly like the entitled, superficial jerk who ruined my life the first time." She pulled out her cell phone.

"Who are you calling?" As if he didn't know. It made him see red.

"I let myself believe you were better than you are." Disillusion put a ragged edge on her voice. "You knew I wanted to come to New York and you used that not just to advance your interests, but to belittle me."

He took her phone and her arm, turning her toward the sofa. "Come here."

"Don't you touch me." She shook free of his hold.

For one second, he stared down a look of genuine violence. He wasn't scared, precisely. He didn't expect she could hurt him beyond a few scratches or bruises, but he was taken aback by how deep her rage ran. How anguished she looked at the same time.

"You dragged me here with a promise of something that means *everything* to me—" She bit her lip, arms straight at her sides.

"Yes. Exactly what is that?" he demanded, looming over her so he could see into her eyes.

She ignored the question, throwing out her

hand in a wild wave. "Just so you could parade me in front of your grandfather as something shameful. I can get that by going home to my father, thanks. Go to hell with your arrangement. *Steve*."

They had more to discuss, but "Last one." He pointed in warning. "I mean that." If he had come away with nothing else from Sebastien's challenge, he had at least reclaimed himself.

"Steve! Steve, Steve, Steve, Steve, Steve, Steve!"

He wanted to crush the word right out of her, but kept himself just this side of civilized as he gave her a deadly stare. "Use the name you call me when I'm inside you."

Her pupils expanded and a shadow of betrayal moved within them, dimming the angry light in her golden eyes. "Don't. Just admit you're a bastard."

"Not by birth, but definitely by nature," he agreed, moving closer. "Now call me by my proper name. My real name, *glykia mou*. Or I'll make you. You know I can." He was pretty sure he could. He had spent most of their honeymoon learning how to wring the prettiest noises possible from her.

Her jaw set and lifted as he came into her space. She glared up at him, mouth tight, hands still fisted at her sides. "Give me back my phone."

"You do not get to call your guard dog every time we have a disagreement."

"It's not a disagreement. You *lied*."

"I told you I wanted to marry you for this." He shaped the air closest to her body, deliberately keeping his hands in the space where the heat exchanged, but they didn't touch. Her nipples peaked as though he fondled her, though. Her breath changed and he knew by the way her thighs twitched that she pulsed in a way that echoed the tightening in his own groin.

"You said…" She swallowed, gaze clouding. "You said you wanted…"

He waited, feeling the pull of satisfaction in the corners of his mouth when she couldn't remember what they were talking about. Neither could he.

"I want *you*," he told her. Truthfully. With gut-wrenching honesty, if she only knew it. "Open your dress."

She breathed loud enough for him to hear it. Her mouth trembled.

"Why are you doing this?" she said with a helpless pang.

He cupped her cheek and stepped close enough to drop his head and capture her lips. No resistance, just pure, hot response as she welcomed him. He stole greedily past her teeth with his tongue, fingers dispatching her buttons with more urgency than finesse.

Her hands went into his hair as her dress fell open. He released her bra and took possession of her breasts, loving her groan of abject pleasure as he found both her nipples and rolled his thumbs over the pert tips.

Bending, he stole a taste of each one, wanting to linger, but wanting other things. The win. Total surrender. He turned her away from him.

"Put your hands on the wall."

She did, breath ragged as she placed each palm flat on either side of the call button on the brushed-nickel panel next to the elevator. As he ran his hands up under her skirt and caught at the lace that was soaked with her response, his breath hissed in, hot and fiery, burning his chest.

He lingered to caress her slippery folds, watching her back bow and shudder, feeling her cling to his light penetration.

"More?" He barely choked out the word. "You want me?"

"Yes." She arched as he brought her skirt all the way up to her waist and caressed the smooth globes of her ass.

"Say it." He ruthlessly clung to control. Of himself. Her. But rationality was disappearing behind stark need. "Ask me for what you want. Ask *me*."

"Use a condom."

He tightened his fingertips into her hips, so aroused by her words of permission he nearly went blind, but fought it, not certain he could keep himself from taking her without getting what he wanted first.

Then he heard her moan, "Please, Stavros…"

CHAPTER SIX

SHE WOKE ALONE in the bed. The humid scent of a recent shower drifted from the open door of the bathroom.

Her whole body protested when she sat up, muscles aching from exertion, brain lethargic from heavy sleep. She couldn't help a small whimper as she swung her feet to the floor and sat there naked on the side of the bed, feeling profoundly alone.

"Sore?"

She flashed a look into the dark cavern of the walk in closet, heart leaping in surprise. He was naked, but there was no reading his expression or even the tone of that one word. Concerned? Smug? She couldn't tell.

He'd been insatiable last night, but there'd been something in his desire for her that had made him undeniable. She knew there was something in his name, his relationship with his grandfather, something that pierced into the very heart of him.

She had felt him trying to exorcise it last night, as he had immersed himself in their lovemaking, not taking, but giving, again and again. His concentrated attention, his words of praise and pleasure, had been reassuring and compelling, but what had really kept her as lost to passion as he was had been that layer of inner pain she couldn't reach.

Succor. They had sought that together last night.

In the light of day, she still felt flaunted as something substandard, though.

She pulled the edge of the sheet across herself. It was a flimsy shield.

He finished pulling on his shorts and skimmed a white business shirt from a hanger. He shrugged into it as he came into the bedroom.

"I'll start a bath for you. Tell me next time if it's getting to be too much."

She snorted. "How does that go?"

"You say, 'Stavros, it's too much. Go to sleep.'" He moved into the bathroom and she heard the water turn on.

She hung her head in her hands, thinking that he might be able to turn his libido off and on like a tap, but hers wasn't so easily controlled. Not by her at least. By him… God, she hated herself right now, pleasures of the night notwithstanding.

She felt the weight of his stare as he returned. She lifted her head to see him buttoning his cuffs. He moved his sure fingers down the front of his chest.

"It's because you're Greek."

"The lack of stopping sense?"

He snorted. "That, too, since I don't possess any, either, but no. I meant my grandfather's disapproval."

He moved back into the closet, where he stepped into a pair of gray pants. He came out threading a belt through the loops, then stood before her as he tucked in his shirt.

"He's the son of an immigrant. Loves everything about being American. My father was visiting relatives when he met my mother. She's very traditional and wanted us raised in Greece. My grandfather wanted us here, so my father could help him expand the pharmacy chain his own father had started. They were developing laboratories, chasing patents." He zipped and buckled. "There was a lot of push-pull between them."

He fetched a blue tie and tied it without a mirror, inscrutable gaze fixed on her.

"After my father died, my grandfather brought us here and closed the door on Greece. My mother went back to see relatives every year and I've been to Athens for business, but my stint as your pool man was my first trip back to our island. My sisters and I spoke Greek to each other as a small rebellion growing up, and I purposely hired a Greek PA so I could keep up the language, but my grandfather has always insisted we speak to him in English. He wanted us to be American and made us answer to our American names. Steven. I've always hated it."

He disappeared into the bathroom and the rush of water stopped. He came back and smoothly picked her up.

"What— I can walk!"

"You can't sit there naked and not expect me to want to touch you, *koukla mou*."

"I wasn't inviting you to."

"No, you were remembering how angry you are. You probably wouldn't have let me touch you at all if I had given you a choice." He gently set her on her feet beside the steaming tub.

She hugged herself, feeling horribly exposed, standing there naked, staring at his tie, knotted perfectly. All of him was perfect. On the surface anyway.

His thumb touched the corner of her mouth where it tugged down.

"I wasn't throwing you in his face so much as asserting my will. That always annoys him. I want you, Calli. I think I've made that obvious."

"And I can't resist you. A match made in heaven. For *you*." She hated that she was so defenseless with him. She was raw and vulnerable while he had everything.

He made a noise and took her jaw in his strong hand. His touch was gentle as he forced her to look up at him. His thumb scraped lightly across her tender mouth.

"He and I have a contentious relationship. I can't tell you the number of times he has threatened to disinherit me—which means yanking the financial rug from beneath my mother and sisters. So I do as he wishes, but in my own way. Yes, I knew he would be angry that I'd gone to the island to find my wife. I didn't do it to hurt or humiliate you, though."

"You still accomplished both of those things." She pulled out of his touch. "But it's only for six months." She could endure it. What was a few months of insult against six years of missing her son? She stepped into the tub and lowered, exhaling as the warm water closed over her. She brought her knees up and hugged them.

Stavros hesitated with his hand in the air before he let it fall to his side.

"I have to go. I've been away from the office too long and I'm holding my grandfather to his promise, now that I've fulfilled his demand." His mouth pulled up, but he didn't show his teeth. It wasn't a smile. "Enjoy the city today."

Stavros deliberately went to his grandfather's office—the one he would claim, now that he was married. He arrived before the old man and waited there for him.

He hadn't lied to Calli. He had a ton of neglected work to clear up, much of it due to Sebastien's challenge. He should be at his desk, but he also needed this quiet few minutes to process his behavior last night. He wasn't an animal, but he'd been completely unable to leave her alone. She had let him make love to her until they were both wrung out, so he shouldn't feel guilty, but he did.

Hell, he knew why he felt guilty. *You still accomplished both those things.* Hurt and humiliation.

He rubbed the back of his neck, arms aching, shoulders aching. He had held back his own pleasure again and again, determined to give her as much as he could. To bind her to him. He had thought she was with him every step of the way, but this morning she had made it sound like she hated herself for giving in to him.

That she looked down on herself for it.

When *she* talked of their six months, she made it sound like she couldn't wait for it to be over.

The door behind him clicked and he turned, ready for confrontation, fueled with Calli's dented self-esteem.

"Measuring the windows for new drapes?" Edward asked.

"You know me so well." Stavros went to the

wet bar to pour the coffee Edward's assistant had started when she'd let him in.

"Long way to go for a wife," Edward said as Stavros brought the coffee over and took the chair in front of the desk.

"I was there on a dare. Sebastien bet me I couldn't go two weeks without my credit cards. A trial run of living without my fortune, if you will. Disinherit away. I'll survive."

"That's a bluff," Edward said confidently, adding under his breath, "Sebastien. When are you going to grow up and quit risking your life at whatever that man suggests?"

"Today," Stavros said, deeply facetious. "I'm married now and ready to take the Dýnami reins."

"Who is she?" Edward sipped his coffee.

Stavros couldn't bring himself to say "nobody." His conscience wouldn't let him reduce Calli to that. "The love of my life, of course."

"Is she?" Edward drilled holes with his hard brown eyes.

It was a familiar look, filled with expectations Stavros could never meet. He wasn't his father. Never would be. It was his fault that his father wasn't sitting in this chair, staring into those eyes.

Stavros had been staring down that expression for nearly two decades, but today, quite suddenly, Calli's voice said in his head, *You're looking in a mirror.*

Which was disconcerting. It didn't even make sense.

Edward swore under his breath before nodding decisively. "Very well. I take you at your word, Stev—*Stavros.*" He flinched as he spoke the name that belonged to his dead son. "Pick a date for my departure and make the announcements. The company is yours."

The moment should have been a triumph. It was anticlimactic. Stavros was used to fighting bitterly to get what he wanted. Edward Michaels rolled over for no one.

So, even as his grandfather told him to put the wheels into motion to replace him, Stavros's knee-jerk reaction was to refuse. *I'm lying,* he wanted to say. *Fight me. Don't let me have it. Tell me I don't deserve it.*

He really was a perverse jackass.

He made himself stand and shake his grandfather's hand.

When had they last shaken hands? The old

man's skin felt papery and his grip wasn't as strong as it used to be.

Quite suddenly, Stavros felt like a bully, like he was taking something from someone weaker.

"Thank you," Stavros said, disturbed, and left.

They had formal photographs taken on Friday morning, ones that would accompany the press release that afternoon. Immediately afterward, Stavros drove them to the family estate, Galíni, which was Greek for *tranquility*. The mansion, nestled on groomed grounds and surrounded by eighty-some acres of forest, was set apart and quiet, and it screamed of tasteful extravagance.

At only fifty years old, the house seemed even older, given the charm and attention to detail. Calli walked into a foyer of mosaic tiles and a stained-glass skylight over a grand staircase. "Only" ten bedrooms, Stavros told her, but each had a private bath, balcony and small sitting room. More of a suite, she deduced, as he showed her to the one they would share. He suggested she change into swimwear since they would join his sisters by the pool.

They spoke to his mother first. She was a stunning woman who welcomed Calli warmly. By the time they went outside to meet his sisters, who also greeted her with delight and natural curiosity, Calli was beginning to feel like a terrible fraud.

"You should tell them," she said to Stavros when they changed for dinner.

"Tell who what?"

"Your family. That I'm not...real. I mean, they acted so surprised. Shocked, actually. Like, even though your grandfather told you to get married, they didn't expect you would."

His mouth twitched. "He and I are renowned for our power struggles." It didn't sound like a lie, but she sensed it wasn't the whole truth.

"I meant that they seemed to think you wouldn't get married ever. Not for any reason." She waited, but he let that speculation hang in the air. "Is that *true*?" she finally prompted.

"Yes." He said it flatly. "But he was adamant he wouldn't hand over the reins until I had a plan for the next generation. I found a workaround." He waved at her.

She wanted to ask why he was so dead set

against marriage. Didn't everyone want to find a mate and form some kind of lifelong commitment?

But his dismissal of her as a "workaround" made her feel insignificant all over again. Like the fake she was.

"Well, they're tripping over themselves to be nice to me, acting like you must have really fallen for me. You should tell them it's not like that and they shouldn't get attached. Otherwise it will be hard when it's over."

"Is this because my sister offered to show you around the city? She paints. She loves walking around with a camera, scouting new subjects and locations. That is why you married me, isn't it? To see the city?"

Calli kept to herself that she could care less about sightseeing. As he glanced over his shoulder at her, she turned to fetch a different bra from the drawer, even though the one she wore was perfectly fine.

She let go of that conversation and was happy when they returned to the penthouse the next afternoon so they could attend their first public function as husband and wife.

A whirlwind of social engagements kept them

busy for the next two weeks. They barely had a moment alone outside the bedroom, but at least she was able to advance her search for Dorian.

During the day, when she had the privacy of an empty penthouse, she stalked her paramour online, refreshing her knowledge of his family, searching his online photo albums for a six-year-old boy—all to no avail. If Brandon's relatives had taken him, they kept their privacy settings locked down tight. The connection wasn't obvious.

She made do with memorizing where Brandon grew up and where he had gone to school—Yale—along with the year he'd graduated and the names of his classmates and social circles. He bred thoroughbreds for racing, so there were a lot of references to tracks and derbies. She had just missed the Belmont Stakes and any chance of "bumping into him" there, damn it.

His family had made their fortune during prohibition, she learned, then turned their name into blue-blood, upper-crust American aristocracy. His father was a lawyer turned senator, his mother a homemaker and charity fund-raiser.

They attended church, belonged to the right clubs, and knew the right people.

They *were* the right people. Four years ago, Brandon had kick-started his own political career with an interim council position. During the election, rumors had swirled about gambling debts and a thrown race, but they hadn't been proved. He was engaged to the daughter of a Washington insider and they lived in Manhattan. He had his sights set on the next election cycle for state representative and was currently on vacation at Martha's Vineyard.

If she could have gone there, if she could simply show up on his doorstep and confront him, Calli would have. Sadly, her previous attempts to contact him had resulted in cease-and-desist orders. A surprise face-to-face on neutral ground was her only choice.

She moved through the various cocktail parties and art exhibits, the ballrooms and living rooms, feeling as though she was playing one of those tile games that shifted one to make room for another. As she went along, she made a mental note of each name, trying to find a connection to Brandon, trying to figure out how she would rearrange these smaller abstract pieces into a bigger, clearer picture.

It wasn't easy when she also had to contend with sugar-coated glares of hostility from all the women who had thought they had a chance at the most eligible bachelor in America. If she had a dollar for every "Congratulations" that dripped poison, she would be as rich as her husband.

As for her marriage, it was the furthest thing from what she had imagined for herself. She hadn't aspired to marry, but when she had imagined such a thing, it had always been a love marriage that included romantic acts of intimate sharing, physical and emotional.

With Stavros, sex was a kind of delirium, the intensity growing rather than abating as time wore on. It was disturbing. Each morning, after giving up another piece of her soul to him during the night, she shored up her inner walls and distanced herself as much as she could.

If he noticed, he didn't let on. Perhaps it didn't bother him. He was focused on work and the new responsibilities he had taken on. He didn't talk to her about it and she didn't ask. She played her part, pretended she didn't feel the daggers or overhear the gossip about herself in the ladies' room. She went shopping when his sisters suggested she join in, and attended lunch when his mother invited her, all without prying beyond what they offered openly. Not because she wasn't curious. She longed to know more about her husband, but she also knew it was pointless. This was temporary.

She was here to find her son. If the emptiness of her marriage made her sad and bereft, well, she had lived in that state for a long time already. She could handle it.

Then finally, a breakthrough.

"I'm sorry," she said as she processed what the man next to her had just said. "Did you say your old rowing team would be there?"

"From my Yale days, yes. The regatta is our annual get-together. Heavy fines if you don't show for the kick-off party." He touched the side of his nose and winked. "We all have to sail with a hangover. Otherwise it's not a level playing field."

Hilarious. She wondered how many people drowned each year.

"What a lovely tradition," she said with the social grace she had learned while hosting for Takis and had honed as Stavros's wife. "Who are your teammates? Have I met any of them?" Her heart began to thud and roll, like paddles hitting the water and pushing through the weight of waves.

Stavros couldn't take his eyes off the light in Calli's face—and his captivation had nothing to do with how attractive she was. Rather, it did, but it had its roots in the opposite side of admiration. Jealousy.

"What were you talking to Hemsworth about?" He skimmed off his tuxedo jacket and draped it over the chair near the window.

"Why don't you hang that?" She moved to do it.

"I pay the housekeeper to do it. She checks to see if it needs mending or cleaning. Leave it and answer the question."

Calli let go of the jacket and stiffened at his tone. "*Wally* Hemsworth?"

"Yes. You lit up like a Christmas tree. He was soaking it up. That was his wife with him, you know."

"Are you accusing me of flirting with a married man? In front of his wife?"

Her wide-eyed shock seemed genuine, but he only raised a brow. That was exactly what it had looked like she was doing. He still didn't know why she had married him and it was beginning to eat at him.

Her jaw moved in a small flinch. She slid her lashes down in what might have been an attempt to disguise hurt. She was the queen of disdain when she spoke, though.

"Last I checked, I was already married to the richest man in the city. What could Wally Hemsworth possibly have to offer beyond that? More sex? I don't think that's possible, is it?" She dropped her jewelry into a dish on the vanity.

"Is that a complaint? Am I making too many demands? You *respond.* If you ever turned me down, I might be able to control myself." He used a facetious drawl, but there was a hard core of truth in there. She flowered every single time he touched her and it was too enthralling to resist.

But that was all they had. Sex. He hadn't expected to find that infuriating, but it grated like sand in an oyster, always there, growing with layer upon layer of attempts to be ignored. She navigated a social event with ease, but gave up little about herself. When people asked him about her, he had few answers.

It left him feeling something he hadn't experienced even when he'd been in Greece, living on pennies. *Insecure.* He wasn't sure of her. It kept his gut in a state of tension and his libido at ten, constantly needing to reinforce their physical connection to ensure she was his.

His frustration sharpened his tone. "Then what were you talking about?"

"Nothing," she insisted, pulling the tie that had scooped her hair over her shoulder. "We talked about his time at Yale and the regatta next week. You said we were going to that, right?"

Her gaze ricocheted from the mirror to his like a bullet.

"Yes. Why?"

She jerked a shoulder that didn't come off as casual. Not at all. "It sounds fun."

"Does it." His mind raced, looking for the missing puzzle piece. "Are you eager for some salt air? Because I notice you don't leave the apartment unless we have an engagement. Even then, you're resigned, not excited. I thought you married me so you could explore New York?"

She kept her back to him, gaze down, face stiff. "When I thought about living here, I always expected I would have to work. Since I don't have a job, I have no reason to go out."

"My sister said you turned down a shopping trip the other day."

"I didn't need anything. I wasn't trying to avoid her. I invited her to lunch."

She peeled off her gown, exposing her mouth-watering figure in a set of black lace shot with silver threads. A deliberate attempt to sidetrack him? If so, it was working. The way her thong framed her ass cheeks was positively erotic and nearly wiped his brain clean.

"Do you really want me to become BFFs with her? Maybe you should tell your family that this is a temporary thing, so they'll stop trying to form a relationship with me. That's why I don't enjoy our evenings out. I keep meeting new people, but a few months from now, I'll never see them again."

"You love to throw that in my face, don't you?"

"What?"

"How temporary our arrangement is. Is that

what you were doing with Hemsworth? Putting your next paycheck in place?"

"For God's sake, no! And do you have any idea how offensive you're being? Every time we're out, I have to face ugly looks and snide remarks about how I'm your quaint little wife from the old country. I lack taste and polish. I'm a social climber. Your grandfather forced you to marry me, since you couldn't possibly have *chosen* me."

"Who said that?" He scowled, instantly affronted on her behalf.

"Do you think I bother to learn the names of the cats in the powder room who make sure I overhear them? *Do* let me put their curiosity to rest, though. How *do* you bring yourself to sleep with such a filthy immigrant?"

"Who said *that*?" His blood nearly boiled out his ears.

"You have quite the reputation. Did you really work your way through a sorority house in a weekend? Because that makes you quite the hypocrite for objecting to my *talking* to one other man."

She swung away and charged into the closet. He heard a drawer open and slam shut.

He swore and pinched the bridge of his nose. He had done some tremendously stupid things as a young man. He doubted he would earn any points by telling her it had been a bet and a dare, and the house had been only half full because the girls who weren't interested in testing his stamina had left.

"You should have told me that was happening," he said when she reappeared in a decidedly unsexy T-shirt and leggings that sent a loud message about her receptiveness to his advances tonight.

"Why? Those women are nothing to me." She hugged herself in the defensive way she did sometimes, like she was huddling against more rain than a person should be forced to endure. "In a few months, I'll never see them again. I'm not throwing that in your face. I'm reminding myself why it doesn't matter. I don't have any claim on you. This isn't my life."

His throat clogged with words, but he couldn't articulate them, couldn't agree or disagree.

"Our arrangement is a trade-off." Her brow flinched. "What do I care what small minds think of me, as long as I get what I want?"

"What *do* you want?" It wasn't the money he had promised her. It wasn't the most exciting city in the world.

For a moment she looked stark with hopelessness, then turned away. "What do you care, so long as you have what you want?"

She didn't wait for his response, only went into the bathroom to brush her teeth.

She made a good point. He stood there listening to the water run, wondering why he *did* care. Wondering why it felt like he *didn't* have what he wanted when, to the outside observer, he had everything.

CHAPTER SEVEN

CALLI WAS SO keyed up, she could hardly think straight.

She had obsessed over every detail of the coming evening. Her gown was the most quietly powerful in the closet, dark blue with an empire waist and a sheer white overlay on the bodice, suggesting royal elegance. She usually did her own makeup, but today she had splurged at a local spa, spending some of her allowance on a stylist who did her hair, as well. Wearing her tallest shoes, she was flawless and proud.

In the mirror.

Inside her clammy skin, her bones rattled with nerves.

Brandon, she would say, looking him right in the eye. *You probably don't remember me. We met years ago and I was deeply in love with the boy who left Greece with you. Dorian. How is he? Where is he?*

It almost didn't matter what he said or did after that. She just wanted to see his face. She wanted him to know she wasn't going away this time. He couldn't pretend he didn't know her, couldn't pretend they hadn't made a baby.

He couldn't even pretend ignorance about the way the adoption had happened. Letters had been sent since then. He *knew* she hadn't consented to the surrender of custody.

The jig was up. *Now* things would be different.

After tonight, she would finally have some answers.

It made her hands feel cold and disconnected from her body. Her heart raced and tripped in her chest. Her mouth was dry, her stomach in knots.

Nervously, she swept open her phone and checked Brandon's social media profile. His last post had been an exchange of comments with Wally Hemsworth, demanding Wally pony up a drink that was owed.

She scrolled to Brandon's profile picture, taking in the subtle changes six years had wrought. It was a professional headshot suitable for a politician. Handsome, she supposed.

Did her son resemble him? Her?

"Who's that?"

Stavros's voice startled her so badly, she let out a small scream and dropped her phone.

Stavros swept down to pick it up off the carpet and turned it over. His dark brows lowered into an accusatory line. "Brandon Underwood?"

It was Wally Hemsworth all over again. It was her father, with his repulsed glare as he pronounced her loose and shameful. She looked away from the sharp query in Stavros's eyes.

"I'm just—" She held out her hand, unable to think of a suitable excuse. Her hand shook. She swallowed. "Can I have that, please?"

"Do you know him?"

"Do *you*?"

"We cross paths sometimes." He didn't give her back the phone. The silence became deafening.

"I knew him a long time ago." She wiggled her fingers.

"Have you been in contact with him?"

"No."

He looked at the screen as though deciding whether to check her messages.

"I haven't," she insisted.

"This is it, isn't it? The reason you wanted to

come to New York." He tilted the screen. "He's the tourist. The one who got you kicked out of your home. You're still carrying a torch? You seriously married me to get to him?" His voice tightened. "That's beyond obsessive."

"It's none of your business, Stavros." She held out her hand.

"You're my *wife*."

"By contract. You got what you wanted. Now give me what I want." She pointed at the phone, even though the phone had nothing to do with it.

He let his hand drop to his side, keeping the phone while he looked at her like some kind of veil had been pulled away and he didn't even recognize her.

It made her squirm, but she brushed aside whatever he was thinking of her. Her palms were sweating with anxiety. Tonight was her night. She *would* have it.

"I have to smile at your past lovers every time we go out. You can get through one night seeing mine."

"Like hell I do. He's *engaged*."

"I just want to talk to him." She stepped forward to take her phone.

He pulled back, yanking on her heartstrings with the movement so every part of her stung.

"Give me that."

"No."

He'd bought it for her, so she could hardly protest that it was hers. Tears smarted behind her eyes. She shrugged, trying to keep her control from shredding while her inner trembling grew worse.

"Fine. Keep it." She moved to pick up her handbag and made sure her credit card was in it. "Are we going? Or am I asking the doorman to call me a cab?"

"We're not going anywhere. You lied to me, Calli. That was your rule. No lies. You didn't tell me why you wanted to come to New York."

"Because it's none of your business."

"It is *literally* my business. My grandfather would love an excuse to back out of the handover. I'm not watching you hook up with your old flame while putting my control of my *business* in jeopardy."

"Stavros." She turned to face him, elbows snapping straight at her sides as she turned her mind from anything but the tiny bridge she had glimpsed, the one that should take her to her son. Why was it starting to look like a mirage? Like the more she tried to reach it, the farther away it became. "This is not negotiable. I'm going to see Brandon tonight. That's happening."

It was the uncompromising tone she had developed as Ophelia's nanny, but Stavros was no adolescent girl.

He pocketed her phone, voice steely. "No. You're not."

"Watch me," she bit out, and turned to the elevator.

"Don't bother calling a cab. One word from me and you're off the guest list at the dinner. You won't be allowed in."

It was a slap. Yet another door slammed in her face before she could take two steps on her quest. She turned.

"Don't. You. Dare." Her ears rang, like they were straining for the sound of Dorian's cry. She could almost hear him. That was why she had woken, that last morning. She had heard him, but it was a distant sound and growing fainter. He wasn't dead. He was moving beyond her reach.

Was that the thump of helicopter blades? Or her panicked heart?

She would *not* go through this again. Not when she was so close this time. Desperation pushed her forward, right up into his space.

"Do *not* stop me seeing Brandon or I will go directly to your grandfather and tell him what a sham this marriage is." The words tripped and hissed, stumbling over a tongue growing thick in her mouth.

"Well, you've tipped your hand, haven't you?" He clasped her arms. "If you're going to make those sorts of threats, I'll put you on a plane back to Greece right now, and tell my grandfather whatever the hell I want."

"Oh, will you!" She slapped at his touch, shaking him off. "Like I haven't been *there* before. For the *same reason*. How dare you try to stop me? How *dare* you?"

"Calm down," he growled.

"Throw me out, then!" Fury erupted from the pit of her being, rising to consume her, just like that midnight confrontation with her father. "You want to tell me my baby is dead, too? Then blacken my eye? It adds a nice touch of ugly desperation when you offer to prostitute yourself. Go ahead! I'll need it out there." She pointed wildly to the window and the bleak streets below.

He recoiled. "What the hell are you talking about?"

She wanted to smash him in the face.

"What baby?" he ground out.

"*My* baby," she cried, hurling the words like hand grenades.

She stood outside herself. She'd been out of control in those early hours of the morning, too. Years of toeing the line around a father who was quick to correct with a swing of his arm had disappeared. She hadn't cared that she was pushing him past his limits. She had only wanted her son back. She had wanted her father to quit saying those awful words about Dorian being dead.

"Brandon *took* him. I've been trying to find him for *six years* and I finally have a chance to confront him, but you—"

She swiped at an irritating tickle on her cheek. Her trembling fingertips came away smeared with black. She was crying. That was why her throat felt like it was made of broken glass. Her chest was under a piano, so tight she couldn't draw a breath that didn't hiss.

Her makeup was ruined and when she looked down, she saw little dots of charcoal had dripped to stain her dress. Even if she somehow pulled her appearance together, she couldn't confront Brandon with her emotions in tatters.

This latest chance was dissolving, just like all the rest. How had she let herself believe this time was different from the others?

Why did it always end like this?

She lifted her gaze, letting Stavros see how shattered she was. How betrayed she was by his refusal to compromise. His imposition of his will.

His act of cruelty.

"I got you what you wanted, but *you*… You're just like Brandon. Your precious life has to be protected at the expense of everyone else's, doesn't it? I knew what you were when I saw you, but I still—"

He jerked his head back, expression stunned, like she *had* punched him in the face.

She might have wondered how her words had struck so deeply if she hadn't been so devastated herself.

"I hate you. I hate *myself*."

* * *

He followed her to the bedroom. She had black tears dripping off her chin, and she yanked at her stained gown. Wisps of her hair were coming out of its upswept knot.

"Calli—"

"Leave me alone." Her voice was thick with rejection.

His heart lurched. He was at an utter loss. What the hell? Was this even real? A *baby*?

"Are you going to make me beg? You love it when I do that, don't you? Fine. I'm begging you, Stavros. Please leave me alone."

Her broken words were the flash burn of a Molotov cocktail to the chest, leaving a hot, gaping hole where his heart resided. He stared at the traumatized woman before him and the look in her eyes snapped something in him. Something that had been golden and bright, something he hadn't even realized had come to exist between them, or even how precious it was.

It was gone now. Incinerated.

He could hardly breathe, but he made himself turn and leave. He made himself give her this one little thing she wanted. Had begged for.

Your precious life has to be protected at the expense of everyone else's, doesn't it?

His father had told him to swim for shore. He had said he would be right behind Stavros. But he hadn't been. The waves had been three feet high. After one glance back, Stavros hadn't risked another. His life vest had been the only thing that saved him, buoying him to the surface each time the waves plunged him under.

Calli couldn't know that she had scored such a mortal blow with her words, but Stavros reeled under the denunciation. *He* was to blame for his father's death. He knew that.

He was still as selfish as that boy who had saved his own life at the expense of his father's. Just look at his reaction tonight. He knew what he had with Calli was more than he had a right to. He kept telling himself it was a quid pro quo arrangement. That was how he justified enjoying her. How he justified playing house in a way he had long written off, not feeling entitled to it.

He poured himself a glass of the red wine that was open, bottle clinking against the glass as he relived that moment of seeing her interest in Brandon. Jealousy had seared through him. The depth that those talons had sunk into him un-nerved him and he took a quick sip, wishing it was stronger, strong enough to burn the tension from the back of his throat.

He had ruthlessly shut down their evening be-cause he had felt, yes, that his precious time with her was threatened.

He was still jealous. She had a son. With Bran-don Underwood.

Once again he found himself wondering how his life would have been different if he had stayed on the island. Would that boy be his?

A fresh snap sounded and his palm stung. Red wine soaked past the shards of glass in his skin, changing shade as blood rose to mingle with the dripping liquid.

Stavros swore and went to find the first-aid kit, leaving bloodstains on the tile.

There had been days over the years when Calli had let herself hope. Times when she had a little money saved, or Takis sent a letter, or some other thing happened and she would let herself believe that her time of waiting was coming to an end. She would see Dorian again. Soon.

Then the other shoe would drop. Her dreams would be dashed and she would be overcome with grief all over again, crying so hard she was sure her lifetime allotment was used up.

Each time, once the storm passed, she was left hollowed out and desolate. Then, very slowly, she would gather herself and make a new plan.

So she knew it wasn't over. It would never be over. If she didn't have another chance tomorrow, she would make one for herself the next day, or someday far in the future. She had done this before, too many times to count.

It took courage to work herself up to taking action, though, especially when the disappointment was so profound when it didn't work out. So she didn't try to make a new plan tonight. Tomorrow she would figure out how to proceed. Tonight was for accepting she had lost.

Again.

Footsteps sounded on the stairs to the loft. She remembered where she was, curled up in the corner of the settee in the dark of Stavros's penthouse bedroom. She had let her gown fall to the floor and stepped out of it, then wrapped a blanket around her while she cried. Now she was aching in the aftermath, filled with despair, blinking to focus her swollen eyes on the lights of the city laid out like a carpet of stars below her. Her heart weighed heavily in her chest.

Stavros had threatened to send her back to Greece, she recalled, which didn't sound so bad, actually. Takis would take her in. She could see Ophelia. At least she had that. She was terribly lonely here.

She glanced burning eyes toward the closet, wondering what she should pack. Her brain conjured nothing.

"It's late. I thought you'd be asleep," Stavros said.

She was tired. So tired.

So sad.

"I just wanted to ask him where Dorian was taken." Her voice barely functioned beyond a whisper, flaky and dry. "Where he is now. That's all."

She heard his breath hiss in, like her words had struck and hurt, but what did he know about pain?

"It wasn't about sex or getting back together with him. I would never see Brandon again if I had a choice, but he's the only one who can tell me what happened. His lawyers have been saying for years that nothing even happened between us, but a baby isn't nothing."

Stavros moved to stand behind her. She sensed his hand gripping the back of the settee near her shoulder.

"No," he agreed solemnly. "No, it's not."

"He can't say he didn't know how I got pregnant or by who. I called him and told him it was his. He offered to send money for an abortion. When I refused, he offered to pay me off if I kept quiet. He didn't want his parents to know, but my father contacted them once he realized I was pregnant. He figured they would pay more than Brandon had offered, and I guess they did."

She swallowed, recalling how sordid she had felt by it all, how she had begged her father to stay out of it.

"I didn't want *money*, especially when they said I would have to give him up. I thought Brandon loved me, that he would want to get married, but he just wanted me to go away."

"But he did want the baby?" Stavros spoke low

and level, getting the facts. "He must have, if he took him."

She plucked her words from a maelstrom of deep, twisted emotions. Each extraction was agony. "Since he doesn't appear to have a son, I would say no, he did not want our baby."

"But you're certain he took him?"

"Someone did."

"Who?"

"Exactly." Her voice caught and she had to clear her throat. She snugged the blanket higher around her shoulders and neck. "Dorian was two weeks old and I woke up because I heard him crying. He wasn't in his bassinet. I went to the kitchen and my father was up, even though it was two o'clock in the morning. He said Dorian had died. I mean, really? I ran outside and I could hear a car engine. Our place was near the private airfield and a few minutes later I heard the helicopter. Papa stuck to the story and when I became hysterical, he let loose, then turned me out."

Stavros swore, stark and hard.

"That's when you wound up sleeping on the beach? For how long? You had just had a *baby*."

"Takis thought my pimp had worked me over. He wanted to take me to the police."

"You didn't go? For God's sake, why not?" His voice rang with disbelief, making her shrink all the more tightly into the corner.

"I was scared. Ashamed. My mother was standing by what my father had done. Said Dorian was *in a better place*. But where was the body? I accused Papa of killing him. That's when he really came after me. Not a man who will stand for being accused of murdering a baby, but he had no compunction leaving his daughter for dead on his front step."

"He abused you? Regularly?" His voice was steely and terrifying, making her tremble. She curled even tighter under the blanket.

"Mostly we knew how to keep from making him angry. I was just so upset about losing Dorian."

"Calli." The settee creaked as he leaned over her. "Being beaten wasn't your fault. None of this was."

She flinched at the way he was speaking, throwing the words down on her like stones. She leaned away, not really caring about that part of it anymore anyway.

"Takis took me to the police when I finally told him. By that time, Papa had used the Underwoods' money to buy a death certificate. The police refused to investigate. Takis had his lawyer send a few letters, but the Underwoods stonewalled. They called me an opportunist and said I was deluded." She shivered. "They said if I had a baby, it wasn't Brandon's. That given the way I was behaving, I wasn't a fit mother anyway."

"So you don't know for sure that—" He rubbed his hand down his face. "Do you know if your son is alive?" he asked gently.

"In here." Her voice broke as she touched above her left breast. "In my heart, I know he's alive. Just as I'm sure that Brandon knows where he is. That's all I wanted to do tonight. Ask. But no one wants me to know what happened to my son. Even Takis didn't want me to know, not really. He didn't want me to leave him and Ophelia."

Her voice thickened and the tears threatened to come back, burning hotly and stinging the edges of her eyelids, thickening her throat.

"Calli—"

"I'm really tired." She forced herself to stand, numb fingers clinging to keep the blanket around her while she swayed on her feet. "Do you— Can I pack in the morning? I'm sorry. I'm just really tired." Her legs felt too weak to support her.

"No. I mean yes. I mean, go to bed." He spoke in a flat, gruff voice and followed up with a curse that made her hunch protectively again. "Do you need help?"

"No." She took the few steps to the bed and let herself drop onto it, eyes closed, cocooned in the blanket as she curled into a ball of misery and escaped yet another dark, hopeless night.

Stavros put on a fresh pot of coffee when he heard Calli stir. He was glad to finally have something constructive to do, having made as much progress as he could and was now just waiting until he would have to wake her.

She showered and came into the kitchen as he was scrambling eggs.

She paused when she saw him, face bare of makeup, eyes bruised, mouth pouted. She had slept late, but she looked like she could use another twelve hours. She pulled the lapels of her robe closed, sitting at the island when he set her breakfast there.

"Thank you," she murmured.

He slid her phone toward her. "Takis would like to hear from you."

"Is Ophelia okay?" She picked it up to check her history.

"She's the one who called. She had some questions about cosmetics. I asked her to put me on to him."

"Why?" Her honey-gold eyes flashed up, deeply defensive and wary.

His heart flipped over in his chest. There weren't words sorry enough for the pain he had caused her last night. He swallowed, helpless and furious and perhaps not as regretful as he should be, because she had been going about this all wrong.

He kept all of that to himself, though. He instinctively knew that any sort of strong emotion from him right now would send her shrinking into her shell.

"I wanted to know what steps he had taken to find your son."

Her sooty lashes fell and she set aside her

phone. She tucked her hands in her lap and her voice cooled. "Why?"

He sighed, and pointed at her fork, urging her to eat. "Be thankful I did. My first instinct was to go beat the truth out of Underwood. Takis counseled me to use proper channels."

Actually, he had said, "Be careful. Once they knew she was looking for him, they closed ranks. I hired an investigator who found nothing. Meanwhile, steps were taken that nearly cost me my career, my daughter's future and my ability to support both of them. Nothing that could be traced back, of course, but the pressure stopped when the search was dropped. Calli doesn't know about that and I'd rather she didn't. She castigates herself enough."

That explained why Takis hadn't seemed to try as hard as Calli would have liked. Stavros remembered their wedding day, when Takis had said he had let Calli down.

"I can apply my own pressure," Stavros had told Takis. "And I'm a lot more impervious to threats and retaliation than you are."

"Why do you think I let her marry you?" Takis had said flatly. "I hoped she would ask you for help. Good job on getting her to open up. It took two years for her to tell me. This is not easy for her, Xenakis. She's not as tough as she acts. Use kid gloves."

Stavros saw that. Now. Her shoulders were incredibly slight. She was pale. Her hand seemed translucent and slender as she picked up her fork and nudged a bite of egg.

"I tried proper channels," she murmured. "I need to talk to Brandon face-to-face."

"Calli." He leaned his elbows on the other side of the island, so they were eye level. "Why did you marry me?"

She took a few grains of egg into her mouth and let the fork slide out from her sealed lips.

"So you could come to New York and have a conversation with Brandon? You could have come here for a week and done that years ago. That isn't all you want, is it? Why haven't you spent any of the money I've been giving you?"

Her lashes fell.

"Because you need to bankroll a legal battle. Right?"

"I need to know where he is first. That he's safe." Her gaze came up, fraught and urgent.

"That's the most important thing. If I start with a letter from a lawyer, Brandon won't see it. I can guarantee you they won't even forward it. No one will confirm Dorian is alive. But if I look Brandon in the eye— Don't try to talk me out of this, Stavros!" Her eyes filled as she read his expression. "Is it because you think it will drag your family into a scandal? I won't go to the papers, I swear. I don't want to put my own son in the middle of something public and ugly. I wasn't going to make a scene last night. I had the words rehearsed in my head—"

"Calli." He reached across to cover her hand. "I need you to trust me."

"No!" She stood, yanked the tie on her robe tighter and stood there shaking. "No. I won't and I *don't* trust you."

It was a damned sledgehammer to the chest. He pinched the bridge of his nose. "Calli, listen—"

"No! Damn it, I know I was only seventeen." She pushed the heels of her hands into her eye sockets. "I know he might be better off where he is. He's probably with some rich, married couple who can give him a much better life than I ever could. I know I didn't deserve him." She dropped her hands to reveal the suffering in her eyes. "But I didn't give him up, Stavros. He was *taken*. I have to know he's safe."

He felt her pain in that moment. He felt it like knives in his chest and belly, like a tortuous ache that made his entire being throb. He felt pulled and anchored down at the same time, feet heavy as he went around to her and closed her cold fists in his bigger hands.

"I didn't say you didn't deserve him. Who said that to you?"

She pulled her hands from his and tucked them under her elbows, turning her face away as she fought to hang on to her composure.

He drew her into his arms, but she was as stiff and cold as marble. He set his lips against her temple. "Of course you deserved to keep your own son."

She flinched, pulling back in a way that clawed at him. He wanted to crush her, press reassurance into her so tightly she couldn't doubt it, but she was like spun glass in his arms. Not nearly as strong as she was trying to be, fighting back tears with that jagged, hissing breath. Her whole body was quivering like an animal run to ground.

"I have more resources than Takis," he said in a gentle, yet gross understatement. "The lawyers I hire will hire their own investigators. Good ones. Most important, contrary to what you just said, I am not afraid to use the press as a weapon."

"But what if Dorian doesn't even know he's adopted? It would be horrible to learn something like that on the schoolyard. What if—"

"Don't worry, *koukla mou*. I don't expect it would progress beyond a threat. The Underwoods do *not* subscribe to any publicity being good publicity. That's why they hushed up their son's mishap in the first place. That and they wouldn't want an heir to show up inconveniently in the future, seeking a piece of the Underwood pie. No. Better to place him in a suitable home where they can give him a measured slice, the way aristocracy has done for generations when they have a blue-blooded bastard to contend with."

"Don't call him that!"

"Apología." He drew her in, pressed his mouth to her hair, still trying to assimilate that she was the mother of a child. A fresh wave of jealousy overcame him as he absorbed that she would al-

ways have this connection to Brandon, her first lover. It was far more profound than losing her virginity to some man he'd never met. Brandon would always be a peripheral figure in her life and Stavros couldn't do a damned thing about it except loathe the piece of filth.

"Do you think he's with a family member? Because I've searched and searched online. I can't find a sibling or cousin or any other relative with a boy of the right age."

"Let me put my mothers and sisters on the job," Stavros said drily. "They'll have a list of possibilities in an hour. They know every top-tier familial connection in the country."

"I don't want them to know *this*."

"I don't have to tell them why." He glanced at the clock on the microwave. "But I'd like a starting point for our meeting."

"What meeting?"

"Lawyers, *koukla mou*. They'll be here soon."

"How—? It's the weekend!"

"Yes, they'll ding me for that, along with the fee for the house call, but…" He shrugged it off. "I wanted to let you sleep."

She drew back, brows pulled into a knot of worry. "Why are you doing this?"

"We have a deal, do we not?" *Now* it was quid pro quo and he grasped at the opportunity to justify their arrangement. Keep it going exactly as it was. "As you pointed out last night, I have not upheld my side of the bargain. You could have been more forthright in your reasons, but I am honor bound to give you what you sought when you agreed to marry me."

"No, you aren't," she mumbled, hair falling in a curtain down her cheek as she dipped her head.

"Oh, I am." He smoothed that wisp of hair behind her ear, mostly as an excuse to touch her. "You made a rather harsh comparison last night, *glykia mou.* I am not just like your faithless Brandon. I like being called *that* even less than Steven."

Her mouth quirked in a hint of leavening, but quickly skewed again with emotion. Her brow grew heavy. "I don't know what to say."

"You don't have to say anything. Sit. Eat. It's going cold and you missed dinner last night."

She went onto tiptoe and grazed her mouth against his cheek, filling his head with the scent of her freshly washed skin. Her voice rasped with emotion. "Thank you, Stavros."

She sat down and his tension bled out of him on a quiet breath of relief.

CHAPTER EIGHT

CALLI COULDN'T SEEM to move, barely able to lift her head as Stavros came back from seeing out the lawyers. She was emotionally exhausted. Hollowed out and raw.

But hopeful.

Which terrified her.

"I realize that wasn't easy for you," he said, lowering to sit on the ottoman in front of the armchair where she had huddled and cried, pouring out her soul along with the sordid details of her teenage affair.

"Which part?" She had covered everything, drawn out by the kind, soft-spoken Ingrid while she avoided the drilling glare from Norma unless the older woman interjected with a sharp-voiced question.

Oddly, it was that tag team of hard and soft, compassionate and ruthless, that had reassured her. Takis's lawyer had been at turns overwhelmed, distracted and impatient. Norma, Ingrid had informed her, was a champion of justice. Ingrid believed in her, which was why she worked with her—despite Norma's lack of bedside manner.

That gentle humor and candor had allowed Calli to open up to Ingrid, but shame had colored every word. Shame for how she'd got herself pregnant and how shame had kept her hiding it as long as she could, waiting for Brandon to come back and marry her. Shame that she'd been stupid enough to believe he would and deep, deep shame instilled by her parents when they'd learned. Shame that they hadn't loved her enough to overcome their own embarrassment, rejecting her and refusing to keep Dorian, then shame that she had trusted them. Shame that she hadn't suspected her father could go to the lengths he had. Shame that she had lost her son. Mothers were supposed to protect their babies at all costs, right?

The shame had continued well after she had offered herself to Takis. Askance looks around the island had kept it going as rumors swirled of her giving birth out of wedlock and losing the baby to crib death, then living with Takis as his presumed mistress. She was ashamed that she had taken so long to tell him, to fight for her son, only to lose.

"The part where they asked you for time." Stavros set his elbows on his thighs, hands linked between his splayed knees. "You've already waited too long."

She twitched a shoulder. What did a couple more weeks matter after six years?

"Can I ask— You said that you didn't tell Takis right away because you didn't think you would stay with him that long, and that you were embarrassed, but what made you finally tell him after keeping it secret for two years?"

She sighed and gathered up the balled tissues that had collected in her lap and around her legs. "He asked me to marry him."

"Ah." His hands closed a little more tightly together.

"He knew he was too old for me, but he wanted a brother or sister for Ophelia. We gelled as a family in a lot of ways. For the first time in my life, I felt…wanted. Ophelia was a brat, but she loved me. Does."

She smiled with affection, missing her girl.

Feeling the distance, especially today, when her emotions were so spent and heavy.

"She helped me so much and doesn't even know it. On my worst days, when I felt like an utter failure for not having my son, she would cuddle up to me, or give me something she'd made at school, and I would realize I was the only mother she had. It made me want to…" She cleared her throat. "I always thought… Somewhere out there, someone is looking after *my* child. Ophelia's mother would want to know *her* child was being loved and looked after well. I couldn't rob Ophelia just because I was missing my son. I had to give her my best and hope my son was getting the same from the woman he was calling mama."

She grabbed a fresh tissue and swept it across her damp lashes, impatient with this unending leak. Her eyes were beyond raw.

"I made it clear to Takis that I was saving my wages to go to America, but little things kept happening with Ophelia that made it hard to leave. Every time I brought it up, Takis would offer me more money. I would sock it away, thinking I was buying more time in America, more time to plan my attack, more money for lawyers."

She sighed and propped her head in her hand. It was too heavy for her neck.

"Then we went to Athens for my birthday and he took me out to dinner and proposed. I was stunned. Didn't see it coming at all. And when he told me he wanted to make a baby... I fell apart. It all came out and he was so shocked, but he tried to help and..."

"Didn't get very far," Stavros finished softly.

"You're sorry you picked me now, aren't you?" He had to be, which made her sad. "I should have told you. I just don't like talking about it. It hurts."

"I know."

The concern in his expression undid her. It took those passionate, deeply fascinated feelings she had for him and made them flower into something more poignant and permanent. Love. She had probably been in love with him for a while now, but this was the moment where it blossomed and became real. He knew her deepest secret and didn't judge her for it. He wanted to help her.

She dropped her gaze, trying to hide the glow

of yearning that dawned in her heart and swelled to suffuse her whole being.

"Come here." He leaned to gather her up, then shifted them onto the sofa so she was in his lap. "You worry me when you're looking so vulnerable like that. We're going to find him, Calli. I'm going to do everything I can to make this right for you."

She wanted to believe him. She believed *he* believed it, which was deeply reassuring. Sliding her arm around his neck, she buried her face in his throat, moved beyond words. Her throat closed, trying to hold back revealing how much his support meant to her. How much *he* meant to her.

She turned her lips against his skin instead, telling him with her openmouthed kiss and the small shift of her body how she felt about him.

He stilled and she felt him swallow. He drew back to look down at her, thoughts unreadable when his eyes were slitted like that, his lashes a forested line.

He usually made the advances, but she took the initiative, pressing her mouth to his, letting him know she was interested. Receptive.

He kept the kiss brief, pulling back a little to keep staring down at her in that inscrutable way. "You don't owe me anything, if that's what you're thinking."

That's not what this was, but— Oh, God, now she felt like a fool. Perhaps her messy personal life had completely turned him off. "You don't want to?"

She drew her arms from around his neck, tucking them protectively against her chest. She must look like hell, too. What was she *thinking*?

"Calli." He adjusted her position in his lap so she felt the hardness of his erection against her butt cheek. "That happens when you're not even in the room. All I have to do is think about you. It's inconvenient, if you want the truth. I *always* want you. But I don't take advantage of women when they're at a low point."

"Stavros—" She dropped her head against his collarbone. "I'm not trying to compensate you. I want to feel something besides pain." She let her head fall back. "Do you mind?"

He snorted and gathered her high against his chest as he stood. "In that case, I'm your man."

* * *

Stavros was at a loss as he set Calli on her feet beside the bed. Sex was a playful pursuit for him. A sport. Not the game-hunting kind. More a good-natured set of tennis. He liked to control the play, definitely kept track of how many points he scored and he was always willing to take instruction and hone his skills.

With Calli, a new bar had already been set in terms of intensity and endurance, not to mention sheer level of enjoyment. Plus, given how frequently they came together, he knew exactly how aggressive he could be while keeping her with him through the whole act. It was mind-blowing how great the sex had become with her.

But this was different. There was no room for dominance when she was so completely defenseless. She needed healing, and he was capable of gentleness, but he didn't know how to be tender. Not without opening his heart.

That shift terrified him. He was a man who thrived on risk, but he was taking a huge one here. He couldn't turn away from her, though. If ever there was a time to be selfless, this was it.

A strange instinct guided him, something that

had its origins near last night's jealousy, but wore the flipside of it. Humble gratitude, maybe. A sense of privilege that he could be the man to touch and heal.

His hands moved of their own accord to carefully sweep her hair. As much as the need to consume her gripped him, he ached to absorb her in smaller ways. Savor her. He found himself lingering with his lips against her cheek, appreciating the softness of her skin and the delicate scent that reminded him of Greece.

As he turned her to help her shed her top, he pressed tiny kisses against her nape. They were small stamps of reassurance. He wouldn't rush her. They had all the time in the world.

They didn't, he acknowledged distantly, gut knotting with tension, but in this moment, time was at a standstill. He smoothed his lips against the warmth of her shoulder, murmuring how lovely she was.

She chuckled softly and reached to cup his jaw, turning her head so they were nose to nose, lip to lip.

"We've been speaking English so much I didn't understand you right away," she said in Greek. "I like it when you use our language." She pressed her mouth to his, lips clinging in the way that went straight to his head.

He tamped down on the animal that rushed up in him, turned her and drew her slender form into his front, forcing himself to keep the kiss from raging out of control.

It was incredibly powerful regardless, fracturing all the walls inside him. He tasted the emotion on her lips. The enormity of all that she was, all the expansive feelings she hid within that sweet, calm exterior she showed the world.

He was the only one she showed this side of herself, he realized with a fresh rush of dizzying excitement. This passion of hers, these depths, they were all his. No one else caught more than a glimpse. It made him that much more possessive, yet careful, as he unwrapped the gift that she was. And when they were naked on the bed, he let her press him onto his back and slither her soft form and flowing hair over his skin.

"You're making me crazy," he growled, cradling the sides of her head. Her hair spilled from between his fingers, forming a tent around them as they kissed. The rest of him was a line of primed muscle, holding still, acutely aware of her straddling him, teasing his shaft with her nest of curls, breasts swaying lightly against the plate of his chest. He was damned near levitating, wanting so badly to be in her.

"I want to make you crazy," she told him, smiling the sly grin of a woman exalting in the power of her femininity. She was both beautiful and terrifying. He swelled with pride at being the man who gave her this confidence while he feared what he had unleashed.

He had stopped worrying about his mortality years ago, but in that moment of glorying in the goddess that held him in thrall, he was petrified. At some point, this would end. Not just their faux marriage, but their lives. They would age and die, and this woman was far too precious not to live forever. He was far too greedy not to demand an eternity with her.

If only...

He tamped down the thought. Rather than grow urgent, he slowed his movements even more. Drew out every caress and cherished every sensation. He tasted her gasps of pleasure and listened for the music beneath her skin as he stroked her. He gave himself up to whatever she chose to take, watching, experiencing her wrench of climax like it was his own, even though he held back, stunned by her glorious release as she rode his hips.

Then he rolled her beneath him and gave more. More of himself, more attention and assurance and assuagement. Everything in him was hers. And when he finally gave up the last piece of himself and poured himself into her, as she clenched and cried out her own joy, it was not only the most potent and satisfying climax of his life, it was worth all that it would cost him when he had to let her go.

As if Stavros hadn't already pulled her apart and put her back together a million times, he did it again when he asked her to go to the anniversary party for his friend Sebastien.

"Antonio and Alejandro will be there. They're all good friends. I'd like to see them."

He wasn't saying he wanted her to meet his friends, precisely, but it seemed significant. Although he had introduced her to his family despite their marriage having an expiry date. Maybe he was just as blasé about bringing her into his social circle.

Things had shifted since she had told him about Dorian. Stavros was the same dynamic man who didn't stop working unless it was to make love, but he scaled back their appearances to a few smaller dinners with people she had already met. When Friday came, he drove them out to Galíni, where much of the weekend was spent lazing by the pool with his family, talking about everything and nothing.

As relaxing as it was for her, Stavros kept working, drawing his grandfather into several conversations about this or that initiative.

"You always make Edward sound like such a hard case, but he seemed really supportive of all the things you're planning," she remarked as they drove back to the city.

"Things were a lot different when I was younger. Even a year ago." His expression was difficult to read behind his sunglasses, but she had the impression he was somewhere between perplexed and concerned. "I guess he's retiring from riding my ass along with the rest."

She snickered, but he didn't.

"Why did he tell me to bring you back in one piece from Oxfordshire?"

He scratched his cheek, saying drily, "He might have had reason to ride my ass. Sending me to Greece is one of the tamer things Sebastien has goaded me into."

That made her curious, but now she was thinking about the trip itself. "England seems a long way away," she murmured.

"Norma knows to call if something turns up with Dorian."

The way he spoke her son's name as if he was a real person and not some dirty secret turned her inside out all over again. It made her all the more susceptible to him. She reminded herself daily that he was only holding up his side of their bargain by hiring Norma, but she couldn't help wondering if it was a signal he was growing to care for her.

It had been two weeks since she'd told him, and she jumped every time her phone buzzed with a text or he took a call in front of her. She agreed to the anniversary party simply because she needed the distraction of another weekend away.

Waldenbrook, the two-hundred-acre estate in

Oxfordshire, was certainly a distraction. She nervously double-checked her appearance in the mirror behind the visor as the car slowed to amble up the long drive toward Sebastien's majestic estate house. It was right out of a period drama, lovingly maintained since its erection in Georgian times, and scrupulously groomed for a weekend celebration of their hosts' first wedding anniversary.

"I'm nervous," she admitted as he parked before the waiting footmen.

"Why? It's a garden party with a few friends." He set the brake and turned off the engine.

She bit back a blurted "Pah!" because her door opened.

This particular "garden" would host five hundred "friends" tomorrow night. Of course she was intimidated. The feeling grew worse as they were shown to the suite of rooms that Stavros said he always used, pointing out the ones reserved for Antonio and Alejandro, bringing their bride and fiancée respectively.

Flowers and a basket of wine, fruit, cheese and crackers put the finishing touch on a beautifully decorated apartment with a balcony overlooking the pool and a huge four-poster bed beneath a pair of Gauguins.

"He doesn't greet *me* like this," Stavros said, handing her the envelope from the flowers.

Calli opened it to read their hostess's elegant script.

Calli,
I hope you will join me in the Rose Room for breakfast at eight tomorrow morning. I've invited Cecily and Sadie. I'd like to take this opportunity to get to know all of you better.
Monika

"Don't they know our marriage isn't...?" *Real. Forever.* She handed him the note and gripped her elbows.

"It's only breakfast. If you don't want to go—"

"She's the hostess. Of course I'll go. I just feel like I'm misleading her. It doesn't matter," she insisted, snapping into unpacking her few things. "This is the role I agreed to."

Stavros didn't know what their roles were anymore. When he had first begun parading Calli on his arm, he had experienced simple pride in having such a beautiful woman at his side. She carried herself well and he had enjoyed the lack of politics. She didn't fish for compliments or act possessive. They were already married, so there was no fishing for that, either. It was easy.

Now he knew the pain she hid behind her quick wit and unassuming demeanor. There wasn't a mercenary bone in her, and playing the role of his wife plagued her conscience. It left him seeing her as far more human than he had at first credited her as being. In fact he saw her as quite fragile, which shifted him into the role of protector.

The last thing his friends would call him was anyone's knight in shining armor.

Still, as they moved downstairs and onto the terrace for cocktails with the guests, Stavros stayed close to his wife. She had already introduced herself to Antonio and Sadie, when she had run downstairs in search of the phone she had misplaced.

Sadie was a stunning blonde with eyes that tracked back to her husband as though magnetized, and Antonio gave her the same close attention when she spoke. His friend was in love?

The obvious chemistry surprised Stavros. He

had understood the marriage to be a convenience so Antonio could have access to his three-year-old son.

"You were right," Sadie assured Calli as they chatted. "I checked in with the nanny and Leo is fine. I'm worrying for nothing."

"You're a mother. It's your job to worry," Calli said with a reassuring smile.

All of Stavros's defensive hackles rose. He started to make an excuse to draw her away, but Alejandro arrived with his fiancée. Cecily was a leggy blonde and Stavros couldn't fault his friend's taste. No wonder they had been necking in the hallway when Stavros had brought Calli down. They still wore a glow.

Their arrival defused his tension until he overheard Alejandro murmur something to the waiter about bringing Cecily a sparkling cider. Cecily was pregnant? She wasn't showing, but it explained his friend's sudden desire to marry.

In another life, Stavros would be pleased for his friends and hopeful that all their wives could become as close as they were. As it was, he was too intent on shielding Calli from further heartache. He drew her into a quiet corner.

"I didn't mean to do that to you."

She frowned with incomprehension. "What?"

"It must be hard for you. Talking to women with children. I didn't mean to set you up for that."

"People have kids," she dismissed, sweeping her lashes down to hide her gaze, but he saw her flinch. "Envy doesn't change my situation. They can talk about them and I can be happy for them. That's just life."

Stavros was still worried and was relieved to go back to a familiar dynamic when she turned in early. He retired to the snooker room with the usual suspects, where Sebastien toasted their successful completion of their recent challenge.

Their friend seemed determined to be smug about having "won," even though he was now committed to giving away five billion dollars.

Stavros dodged Sebastien's attempts to make them admit what they had "learned" from their challenge and muttered, "I think your real intention was to get us married off so you're not the only one wearing a ring."

"And I managed it."

"How is yours working out? With your grandfather?" Antonio asked Stavros.

"Most of the handoff is completed," Stavros replied as he circled the table, planning his next shots. "He's officially retiring at the end of the month, staying on the board in an advisory role."

His grandfather was surprisingly comfortable with all the changes, the marriage included. He must know it was a ruse. The old man wasn't stupid, but he had actually asked if Calli was pregnant the last time they'd spoken, saying, "She looks pale."

Since she was on the Pill and they'd only just stopped using condoms, Stavros would have to be superhuman to have gotten her pregnant, but his grandfather had seemed genuinely disappointed to hear she wasn't.

And even though he had long decided his sisters could continue the Xenakis dynasty in his stead, Stavros had felt like he'd let the old man down. Again.

Sebastien was topping up drinks and Stavros heard Antonio say something about being grateful to have found his son.

"I always assumed my grandfather was the fall-back if anything happened to me," Stavros admitted. "He kept such an iron grip, I thought the company would be his forever. Now I see why he was so determined to whip me into shape." He sipped, inhaling the oaky bite into the back of his throat. "And why he held back letting me have control."

The other men smirked, well aware that Stavros had been a loose cannon in his youth.

Stavros was seeing the old man's heavy-handedness in a new light, though. Over the years, Edward had railed on about how people would depend on Stavros for their livelihood and, given the types of drugs they manufactured, even their lives. It had sounded like rhetoric, but as Stavros took his grandfather's chair, he was seeing the old man's perspective more clearly.

All the responsibility was his and it was enormous.

He wasn't one to entrust such responsibility to others without due regard, either. He could appreciate why his grandfather had been so determined that Stavros's father come home to help him run it, and that his grandson prove his dedication.

He kind of understood why his grandfather was

hopeful he would make a baby with Calli, but still felt the kind of empire-building his grandfather had in mind wasn't for him. Stavros was the outlier, the strain of the bloodline that shouldn't be replicated.

He had promised Calli a son, but it was the one she already had.

Calli woke to cold hands pulling her into chilled, naked skin. She reflexively squirmed to get away. "Stav— What?"

"Warm me up." He dragged her into a tight spoon against his damp body. "I asked Sebastien what he wanted for a bottle of sauterne and he threw it in the pool. Bastard." He pressed cold lips to her neck. His hair was wet.

"There's a bottle of wine in that basket," she reminded, wriggling her backside into him, hoping the friction would take the sting out of contact with his cold skin.

"It's not a Château d'Yquem 1921. I need that vintage for a vertical I'm compiling. One more and I could auction it for a million. Do you want to make love?" His hand slid to cup her breast, cool fingers fondling gently.

"Do you?" She rolled to face him and ran her

hand down to where he was hardening. Growing warm and ready.

His response was wonderfully reassuring when she had spent an evening growing more and more aware of how completely she didn't belong in his world. The people here weren't just business contacts, but friends. People he liked.

"Always." He climbed her nightgown up her body, hands caressing along the way.

She moaned approval, slithering against him to help expose her naked skin, opening her legs so he could nestle into place between them.

In this way, at least, she felt confident and cherished. She felt like this was exactly where she belonged.

They fell asleep still joined. He woke when she disentangled herself some hours later and pinned her in place with a heavy arm.

"Where are you going?" His voice was muffled in the pillow.

"Breakfast."

He grunted a noise of dismay. "I can't think about food right now." He let her go and rolled away.

She smirked, showered, then tentatively made

her way to the appointed room. She had taken care with her appearance and wore one of her prettiest day dresses. It had a floral pattern suited to a weekend brunch, but she hadn't realized how much she had begun to rely on Stavros's presence at her side until she didn't have him to lean on.

Sadie was already there. When Calli had met her yesterday, with Antonio, she had thought them an intimidating couple, utterly beautiful in the way Italians managed without effort, then she had realized Sadie was English, but still very poised and elegant.

Cecily arrived. She was a firecracker who was obviously deeply in love with her fiancé. It made Calli feel even more of an outsider to be the only one in a loveless relationship. The women were incredibly warm and welcoming, though. They were the kind of women she would have very much enjoyed developing long-term friendships with, but she held back, knowing there was no point.

She kept the conversation light, mentioning Stavros's midnight swim for lack of other topics.

Monika chuckled. "That's the sort of thing they do. They thrive on challenging each other.

Of course, this most recent challenge takes the cake."

Calli realized all three of their men had been set up to go without credit cards for two weeks. Antonio had posed as a mechanic in Sadie's garage and Alejandro had gone to work as a groom at Cecily's stable.

Calli exchanged looks with the other two women, who both seemed shocked, especially Cecily.

"This is something they do a lot?" Sadie asked, astonished.

"For years," Monika told them. "Sebastien's first real venture was a zip line in Costa Rica. He was in his last year of university. In order to get the company off the ground—pun intended—he sent out invitations to specific students at different universities here and in the US. He chose the risk takers, but the ones with money. He comes across as impulsive, but he's shrewd. He *dared* them to try it, knowing full well most young men can't resist something like that. He made some excellent connections as well as enough profit to start his next business. That original zip line expanded into the extreme sports club they all belong to today."

"What were the stakes in the bet?" Cecily asked Monika, clearly still dumbfounded.

"If Sebastien won, the men would give up one of their most prized possessions. Alejandro's private island, for instance. If Sebastien lost, he promised to donate half his fortune to charity."

"And all three men completed their challenges?"

Monika nodded. "Sebastien will be making the announcement of the donation in a few weeks' time. He plans to set up a global search and rescue team with it, something that's close to his heart given his near-miss last year."

He'd been caught in an avalanche, Calli learned, and his friends had saved his life by digging him out.

The conversation moved along to the horse trials that would be run today.

"Will you ride today?" Sadie asked Cecily.

Cecily was a show jumper, but she dismissed the idea, saying something about preferring to spend her time getting to know the three of them, but she looked out the tall windows at the dew-laden grass and bright blue sky like a prisoner longing for freedom.

Pregnant, Calli suspected, and experienced a pang, then turned her attention to Sadie's question about what she and Stavros would do today.

"I promised his sister I would take some photos of the grounds, but I imagine we'll wind up joining the crowd watching the show."

Calli was still thinking about the club and the bet and whether Stavros was a horseman when she returned to the room.

He was sitting on the love seat, feet propped on the ottoman. He was showered and had pants on, but was barefoot and his shirt was open. He had a cup of coffee steaming on the side table and was flicking through messages on his phone.

"Sunglasses?" she teased. "Feeling poorly?"

"Just a headache. Sebastien wanted us to try some port after we'd been drinking whiskey all night. I know better." He set aside his phone and motioned her to come to him. "How was breakfast?"

"Fine." She let him draw her down to straddle his thighs and splayed her hands across the fresh-washed planes of his chest as she kissed him. He tasted faintly of mint and more strongly of coffee. "Monika told us how the club was started. I didn't realize your swim was the latest in a long line of stunts. What else have you done?"

He let his head relax onto the back of the sofa, expression rueful behind his sunglasses. "Swimming after a bottle is nothing. We're usually rock climbing without gear or scaling vertical ice slopes. Cave diving. Whatever tests of intestinal fortitude Sebastien can dream up. This past winter was a paragliding ski event. I expect wing suits will be next."

"And you'll do it? *Why?* Wait, let me guess. Peer pressure. Listen, if all of your friends jumped off a bridge, would you?" She took on her best nanny voice, fists on her hips, elbows akimbo.

"Too late. We *have*," he drawled, sidling his hands up her thighs under the skirt of her dress. He lightly traced the edges of her thong. "Blindfolded."

She laughed, wriggling with pleasure at his touch, but astounded at his audacity. "Ophelia wanted me to go on a ride with her at an amusement park once. It went upside down so I refused. I can't even jump off the diving board into our pool."

His pool, she recalled.

"You have a healthy sense of self-preservation. Me, I've never had a reason to live, so I push the limits every time."

They both sobered.

"I hope that was a joke." She lifted his sunglasses and saw something dark move behind his eyes. Ghosts? He was looking past her, wearing the agonized look from that day on the spit. He was such a devilish, assertive man, it was easy to forget he had his own demons.

She cupped his jaw in her two hands, waited until his gaze met hers. "You have very good friends and a family who loves you. Please don't say you have nothing to live for."

"I'm not suicidal, if that's how it sounded." His hands tightened on her hips and she thought he might try to set her aside.

"Stavros." She let her weight settle onto him, signaling her intention to stay exactly where she was. "What happened in Greece? The first time."

His jaw hardened.

"I told you my secret," she reminded softly. "I know your father died. How?"

His hands came out from beneath her dress. "I wanted to go fishing and he made me wear a life vest, but didn't put one on himself. The wind came up, we went over and he told me to swim for shore. I did. He didn't make it."

She drew a breath, one of the heavy, aching kind filled with empathy for his terrible loss. Very carefully she let it out. It moved like powdered glass in her windpipe, straining her voice when she spoke.

"You can't blame yourself. Everyone on the island knows how rough the water can be on that side."

"I was never one to do as I was told, but I did that day. The one time I should have rebelled and stayed."

"And drowned yourself? You can't think that."

He set her aside and rose. "I'm hungry. Are you coming down with me?"

She shifted on the love seat, pulling her skirt down and smoothing it, watching him settle his sunglasses into place and button his shirt, firmly locking her out.

Her heart continued to ache. She knew all about guilt and grief, regret and self-loathing. What she didn't know was how to reach for someone trapped in that same bubble and bring him out of it.

"Ophelia texted a while ago. I'm going to have a quick face call with her, then I'll come down. I promised your sister I would send her a few pictures from the grounds. Do you want to walk with me?"

"Find me in the dining room." He closed his cuffs and left.

"Stavros…" Calli was speechless as she stared into the mirror, throat closing above the heavy, cool lump that sat just below her collarbone.

She couldn't even make herself reach for the matching earrings. The prenup had outlined his responsibility for providing a suitable wardrobe and accessories, but she had never expected it to include a square-cut yellow sapphire surrounded by diamonds, suspended from two ropes of flat-linked, twisted gold.

He had put it on her himself, after zipping her gown—which was the most form-fitting she'd ever worn. Burnt red satin plunged from spaghetti straps to show off her cleavage, forming a perfect frame for the necklace. Then the gown hugged her waist and hips, covering her backside like a coat of paint before falling away in a flare of sparkle-dusted silk.

He eyed her, standing behind her reflection. "It suits you. Brings out your eyes."

"It's making them fall out of my head! What do you mean it's *not* on loan?"

"Well, it's not stolen, if that's what you're implying. I was shopping for an anniversary gift for Sebastien and Monika when I saw it. I wanted you to have it."

Many moons ago, she had dreamed of being whisked into a rich boy's world, but that aspiration had long died, replaced with a simple one where she knew her son and he knew her. For the first time in a long time, she wistfully yearned to be part of a man's life, but not for this. She wanted so much more than a cut stone from this man. Things she couldn't bring herself to ask for.

He'd been remote all day. She had tried to respect his desire to retreat emotionally. She did the same all the time, so she didn't try to get past his shuttered expression, had only asked him whether he wanted to take this path or that.

It had been a gorgeous day. From across the grounds, the sounds of horse hooves and cheering carried from the trials they were conducting. Where they walked, the air was filled with the sounds of nature. Birds and bees. A soft breeze caressed her skin and the air smelled sweet and fresh.

They happened across a stone bridge that crossed a brook and she paused to take several photos of the sun slanting through the trees onto the water.

When she lowered her camera, Stavros turned her into his arms. He didn't say anything, only held her close so her ear was pressed to the steady thump of his heart while the run of water moving under the bridge sounded below.

She hugged his waist, offering the comfort she wished she could have given him earlier. Her insides trembled like the leaves quivering and whispering around them. When he kissed her and took her hand, tugging her along in silence, her heart was so loose in her chest she could hardly walk.

It made this gift all the more surprising, yet profound, completely unraveling her.

She made herself turn and press her mouth to his. "I'm overwhelmed. It's beautiful. Thank you."

They didn't speak about his father or anything else very serious for the rest of the night. They made their way out to the marquee that had been set with round tables, white cloths, crystal and china, then decorated with candles and roses.

It was pure magic and Sebastien and Monika were clearly ecstatic in their marriage. They started the dancing, then Antonio and Sadie joined in, making a fetching couple as Sadie's daring black-and-white gown mirrored the crisp tuxedo her husband wore. What must it be like to be so in love? Calli wondered.

Despite how in sync they seemed, however, Calli thought there was a flash of conflict as Sadie said something and Antonio seemed to stiffen.

Before she could decipher it, Cecily came alongside her. She wore a gold affair that made her look like a gilded angel.

"You look stunning," Calli told her.

"So do you," Cecily said, eye catching on the pendant. "Wow. That's gorgeous."

"Oh, um, Stavros gave it to me," Calli murmured, self-conscious as Cecily's expression softened.

"He loves you," she said, and there might have been a glint of despair or longing in her eyes, but her lashes swept down, disguising her thoughts.

Calli bit back protesting that Stavros didn't love her at all and reassured instead, "Your fiancé is obviously crazy about *you*."

"Because of this afternoon?" Cecily made a face and darkened with a small blush. "That wasn't…what it looked like."

It had looked like Alejandro had thrown her over his shoulder and carried her from the horse trials to their room to make love. What else could it be?

The men joined them at that point and they all moved onto the dance floor, at which point Sadie abruptly left.

"Oh. Something to do with her son, do you think?" Calli asked, watching her with concern.

Monika followed Sadie while Antonio moved

off the dance floor and into conversation with Sebastien.

"They'll let us know if it's an emergency," Stavros said, sharp gaze on his friend.

A short while later, Sebastien assured them everything was fine, that the couple had simply gone into the house.

It became a night to remember and Calli knew she always would. She would look back with nostalgia in her golden years to this time when she had been young and married far out of her league, invited to a party she had no business attending, dancing like Cinderella with the most handsome man at the ball.

The man she loved.

"How's your head this morning? Do you need anything?" she asked as they returned to their room after breakfast. He had disappeared in the middle of the night, leaving her to wake alone, telling her he hadn't been able to sleep and wound up having a beer with Alejandro.

She wondered if he had been regretting being so candid with her about his father, but this morning he was his regular self.

"I'm fine. Why? Are you suffering? You only had a couple of glasses of Champagne last night."

"I only asked because I was just about to get my pill and—" It struck her that she didn't remember taking yesterday's. She frowned and hurried into the bathroom to find her makeup bag, quickly spilling out the eye drops she used for a pollen allergy, and the bottle of over-the-counter pain relievers, before pulling out her blister pack of birth control.

Then she said a word she *never* used.

Stavros came to the door. "What's wrong?"

"I always wait until after breakfast." She was shaking, she was so shocked by what she was seeing. "I have it in my head that medication is better on a full stomach. But when I came back up here yesterday morning..." They had talked and she'd been consumed by what he had told her about his father. She had completely forgotten to take her pill and had carried on with the day.

"It's just one," he said as he looked at the dates on the packet. "That's not usually an issue."

"Except..." She swallowed, feeling nauseous. "Before we left New York, I popped out my pill and left it by the sink, then packed this and went down for breakfast. We ran out to catch the flight right after. I honestly don't remember if I went back and took it."

She was almost certain she hadn't. *Damn it!*

When they had first discussed birth control, Stavros had suggested something like a patch or one of those capsules under the skin. She had never used anything before so she had wanted something temporary, to see how her body responded.

Realizing she had missed *two* made her heart plummet through the earth and into the void of space on the other side.

"We've been having unprotected sex." Her voice trembled and she hardly recognized herself in the mirror. She was white as a sheet.

"We'll get a morning-after pill."

"That's for the *morning after.* It's been three days, Stavros." She slapped the little packet down, but it made only a tinny rattle of a noise, nothing resounding enough for the magnitude of this mistake. Her world, already upside down, began to rend and tear at the seams. "What if I'm pregnant?"

His pupils seemed to explode, turning his eyes midnight black.

"Don't you dare say I did this on purpose," she warned through lips that started to buzz. Her throat burned. "Don't you *dare*."

"I didn't."

She pushed past him to the bedroom, pacing, feeling trapped. She could hardly breathe and the pressure in her skull was so great, she cupped the sides of her head.

"I need to think." But all she could grasp was that they'd been having sex without protection. Lots of it. "Why can't I control myself around you? Why am I so *stupid*?"

Stavros had been dodging this sort of thing from the moment he'd become sexually active. He'd always been diligent about protecting himself as well as his partner, using condoms every single time he had sex. He might have a reckless streak, but he wasn't stupid.

Given how adamant Calli had been that she didn't want children, he had trusted her to take her pills. For the first time in his life, he'd started going bareback. He loved it.

Now he was reaping the consequence. And he might have suspected her of doing this deliberately if she hadn't looked so much like a loved one had died.

"Is this really such a disaster?"

He never would have gotten her pregnant on purpose, but by accident? His hunger for her was showing no signs of abating and, as his mind raced through the ramifications, it hit him that an accidental pregnancy could be a really convenient way of prolonging their arrangement. It wasn't selfish. It was *decent*. Right.

"Make another baby with a man who thinks I'm in it for the money? Who plans to divorce me in a couple of months? What then, Stavros? Do I find myself someone even richer than *you* so I can have access to my child?" She was like a cat, swift in her turn and swipe of sharp claws. "*Yes*, this is a disaster!"

"We could stay married," he growled.

"Do you love me?"

He instinctively recoiled. Why the hell would she even want him to?

She made a noise too injured to be classified

as a laugh. A sharp inhale that dragged over razors. "That's what I thought."

"Calli—" He took a step toward her.

She held him off with an outstretched arm. Her fingers were white at the tips and trembled. "I can't do this again. I *can't.*"

"I don't think you planned this," he said through his teeth.

"Yes, you do." Her voice throbbed with such profound defeat it made his heart clench. She looked to the ceiling. "And there I would be, stuck in a marriage with a man who resents me, just so I could be part of my child's life. I'm really making progress on making better life decisions, aren't I? God, I hate myself right now."

"Calli." He tried to take her by the arms, but she shrank away.

"Can you..." Her voice thinned to nothing and she swallowed. "Can you go arrange the car or something? I need a few minutes."

CHAPTER NINE

THEY BARELY SPOKE all the way back to New York. It wasn't an angry silence, just a thick, significant one. They had no sooner landed and she picked up a text from his sister, reminding Calli she had promised to help with her art-exhibit preparations.

While Stavros's middle sister played an active role in the company, coordinating the many women's health interests, his youngest sister painted. Beautifully.

"No, you have to come," she insisted when Calli tried to get out of it. "You had such a good eye for that mat on my seascape."

Calli had had dumb luck when she had set a sample next to the painting, picking up an understated tone so the entire piece popped in a fresh way. She had only agreed to help with the rest of the framing because she hadn't known how to say no nicely.

"You have to tell them," she said to Stavros when she got off the phone. She meant that he had to explain their marriage was temporary.

"We don't know, do we?" he said without inflection.

Even without shades of anger or blame, it was an arrow through the heart.

She had stopped taking the pills altogether and was waiting for her cycle. Please, God, let her get her period. And since she didn't want to take any further risks of a pregnancy, she supposed disappearing for a few days to the family estate and not sleeping with her husband was a good thing. At least it was something to occupy her mind, rather than obsessing over the child she had and the imaginary one that terrified her because she couldn't say outright that she didn't want it.

She returned to the penthouse a few days later, in time to accompany her husband to his grandfather's retirement party. Once again, she felt like the biggest con artist alive when Edward Michaels singled her out for praise.

"The recent addition of Calli to our family has been a breath of fresh air. I have often believed I knew better than my grandson, but in marrying her, he has proved to me his decisions are sound."

Everyone chuckled while Calli stared at the single drop of red wine that stained the table-cloth in front of her.

"I miss my son every single day," Edward continued. "But I could not be prouder of the heir he gave me in his stead. I know the future of Dýnami is in good hands and I have no qualms leaving it for him to steer."

Stavros seemed a little stunned by what sounded like heartfelt praise. He made a warm and respectful toast, his voice just a tiny bit unsteady. Most wouldn't have noticed, but his mother leaned in to say, "Those two. All I ever see when they're at each other's throats is my husband. They act like they hate each other, but their love runs so deep..." She blinked and small tears hit her lined cheeks.

Calli waited until the applause had died away, then asked, "Did Stavros fight with his father?"

"Oh!" She rolled her eyes. "He was the most headstrong boy. Even before he could speak, he was challenging the both of us. I honestly didn't know what to do with him. And he has never forgiven himself for the accident. I genuinely feared for what he would do to himself without a strong man in his life. When Edward said he wanted to bring us here, of course I went along. It was my children's future. I didn't agree with everything he did, of course. He was hurting, too. We often had words about his decisions."

"In front of the children?"

"Oh, goodness no. The Xenakis men do not enjoy being challenged in front of an audience. They will dig in just to be perverse. No, you pick your time and attack when they least expect it." She made a jabbing motion, as though wielding a pocketknife. "A little advice from a mother who knows." She winked.

Calli chuckled, surprised by this sly side in such an elegant woman. "Stavros told me Edward refused to hear Greek in the house."

"Because our English was terrible! If we were going to live here, we needed to assimilate. Before my husband died, I was so afraid he would take me away from everything I knew, but even I agreed with Edward when it came to giving the children their best advantage. Stavros likes to make out that Edward is some kind of tyrant, but…"

"It takes one to know one?" Calli guessed.

His mother laughed with great enjoyment.

"You've met my son! If he only knew the number of times Edward begged me to take him back to Greece and leave him there." She smiled, but it wobbled. "We used to laugh and cry then, both of us missing my Stavros so badly."

Calli squeezed her arm and tilted her head against the woman's shoulder in a show of compassion.

Stavros returned to their table, brows raised in query as he saw the affection between them.

"We're bonding," his mother said, catching at Calli's face and pressing a kiss to her cheek. "Your grandfather isn't the only one who is pleased with at least *one* of your decisions."

He made some dry remark and the evening continued, but he brought it up when they came into the penthouse after midnight.

"What were you and my mother talking about?"

"Your father. And that she didn't regret bringing you here because she thought you needed your grandfather's influence growing up."

He made a face, one that suggested he might have to reluctantly concede that.

"I'm going to bed," she said, and halted when he said, "Where?"

She turned back, not saying anything. She'd been sleeping in the guest room.

He sighed. "I can wear a condom."

"I won't relax until I know."

The restless look he gave her made her skin tighten. He was thinking about seducing her.

"Don't." It was more plea than order and made him look away.

He hissed out another breath. "Go to bed, then."

Stavros had mountains of work ahead of him, now that he had achieved the pinnacle position in the company. He ought to be immersing himself in it, but found himself with palms flat on his desk, staring discontentedly at the email from Norma.

A letter was forwarded a week ago to the family we believe adopted Dorian. No response yet.

A letter. What kind of letter? To whom exactly? If he was this impatient for answers, he could only imagine how Calli felt.

Calli. He hit Forward on the email, sent it to her, then sat down, prickling with tension. Along with due process, Mother Nature was also taking her time providing news.

Did he want her to be pregnant? It meant they could take up where they'd been and he could keep her longer than a few months.

Not that she was as warm to the idea.

Do you love me?

He had shied away from answering when she had thrown the question at him and still wasn't ready to explore what he felt toward her. It didn't matter. He couldn't ask for her heart either way.

His phone buzzed, snapping him out of his introspection.

He started to set the device to Ignore, but saw it was an unfamiliar number. A premonition made him swipe to answer. "Yes?"

"Mr. Xenakis? It's Ian. The weekday doorman at your building. I see there's a notation on your account that you'd like to be notified if—"

"Underwood is there?" Stavros nearly leaped out of his skin.

"No, sir. But a woman was here in the lobby just now. Wanda Abbott. She asked me to ring your wife, but Mrs. Xenakis came down before I could reach her. She was going out, but I overheard Mrs. Abbott say she and your wife shared a connection through Mr. Underwood. Your wife took her upstairs. I wasn't sure if that was something you wanted to be informed about?"

"Definitely," Stavros said, already on his feet and striding for the door.

Calli was grateful when Wanda Abbott refused coffee or tea. She was shaking too much to pour so much as a glass of water without soaking herself in the process.

Wanda wasn't doing much better. She wore a tailored pencil skirt with a classic sweater set, looking very much an Underwood, even though she explained that she was only a second cousin by a half sister who had married into the Underwood family. She had at least fifteen years on Calli and even though she was perfectly made up and obviously took very good care of herself, she looked every one of those additional years. Her lipstick stood out on her pale features and her eyes were not only weary but tortured.

"I had no idea there was anything about the process that wasn't completely aboveboard," she said after dropping the bombshell that her son,

James, had been adopted shortly after his birth six years ago. "I knew Brandon had fathered him, but we were told the mother had given him up because she was too young. Brandon was only nineteen. I understood why he wasn't ready to be a parent. I had had surgery in my teens that left me sterile and we wanted children so badly…" Her eyes filled.

"My signature was forged," Calli blurted, needing to impress that into the woman.

"So the letter said. It didn't even occur to me such a thing could happen. I was just too happy to have a baby." Wanda's gaze pleaded with Calli for understanding. "We had already been on wait lists with agencies for several years. I didn't take him because the Underwoods set up a trust for him. I wanted *him*. He was such a gift."

Calli searched Wanda's expression, seeing again that plea for understanding. That vulnerability that a baby created in his mother. She probably wore the same expression. *Don't take him from me.*

"Brandon had his whole life ahead of him, they said. A career in politics. That's why they wanted us to keep James's paternity confidential. Brandon's mother comes to see him a few times a year, but not even my sister knows." She dug in her handbag for a tissue, pushed it up against her nose. "When the letter from your lawyers arrived, I was beyond stunned. Devastated."

"I tried once before—"

"So my husband admitted, once I showed him the letter. He said the Underwoods would make it all go away, that they had before. He was furious I opened it. I thought it was about whether we could access James's trust for our daughter's hospital bills. I haven't been myself since she was diagnosed."

"I— What? What do you mean?" Calli pinched her clammy fingers between her knees.

"Our youngest has leukemia. We're not... Well, we're trying everything. It's been difficult." Her eyes filled. "And then to get this news, that we might have to fight to keep James—" She choked and jammed her fist against her mouth.

Calli felt as though she stared down a train, but she was paralyzed. Couldn't move. It was going to flatten her and leave her in pieces, but she was tied to the tracks, unable to avoid it.

"My husband is going to kill me for coming

here, but I had to. I had to tell you that I didn't *know*. I would never do that to someone. And I came to beg you, Calli. *Beg you*. You have every right to want to see James, but now is such a bad time. I'm trying so hard to keep things normal for him. He's usually such a happy boy, but lately he's been acting out and he's not sleeping… He's worried about his sister."

The train whistle filled her ears. The clatter of its wheels grew deafening.

"He knows he's adopted. I've braced myself for this sort of thing, always imagining I would graciously welcome his birth mother into our lives…" Her tears overflowed and her shoulders began to shake. "I knew people's feelings could change. But I just can't do this right now. And if you started picking apart the adoption, tore him from the only home he knows… It could do lasting damage. I'm begging you not to do that to him, Calli."

And there it was. At least now she knew he was loved. He had a mother who would do *anything* to spare her son pain.

"Could…" Calli had to clear her throat. "Could I see a photo of him, at least?"

* * *

Stavros was damn near propelled up the elevator by fury alone. It coursed through him like rocket fuel. The door opened and he charged into the penthouse to the anticlimactic sight of Calli curled up in the armchair, looking at her phone.

"Where is she?"

"Who?"

"Underwood's minion."

She was inordinately pale. Her eyes were rimmed in red, but there was a strange acceptance in her. She looked sober and grave, but resolved. Like one of those religious icons who accepted life's brutality with grace and humility.

"He did go to a loving family." She held out her phone. "She gave me some photos. He looks really happy."

Stavros took it and glanced at a boy with a cheeky grin, his eyes endearingly familiar with their brown-gold color. He swiped to the next one and saw the boy with his arm looped around the neck of a fuzzy-headed, brown-skinned toddler.

"That's his sister. She's sick. Really sick." She took back the phone, swept to another photo, adding in a small voice, "I hope he doesn't lose her. It sounds like they're really close."

"She might be lying," he warned, still battle ready.

"She's not." She swiped for another photo, gaze greedily eating up the image of her son. "She said she would send me updates. That she would try to find a way for me to meet him, but that it probably wouldn't be until they knew what was happening with her daughter."

"You're going to accept that?"

Her gaze came up. "She *begged* me, Stavros. She doesn't have any pride where his well-being is concerned. Mothers sacrifice themselves for their children. The most loving thing *I* could do for him, as his mother, is not pursue my own interests over his. He's in good hands. At least I know that now." She swiped the inside of her wrist against her cheek, clenched her eyes hard then opened them wide, trying to clear the wetness so she could see the screen.

"Calli." He sat on the ottoman and reached to circle her ankle with a comforting grip.

She clicked off the phone and tucked it against her breast. The sound was oddly loud. Significant.

"I'm not pregnant."

A wash of something went over him, far more profound than disappointment. Dread. Portent of pain.

"I see." He didn't know what else to say. He felt sick.

"It's for the best," she said without inflection.

His hand was still on her ankle, but he felt as though he was waving his hand through smoke, trying to catch at her. She was nothing but vapor.

"I think…" Her brow flinched and she cleared her throat. "I think it would also be for the best if we ended things here. Now." Her gaze came back to focus on him, but it held an emptiness that made a protest rise in his throat.

"You agreed to six months." His voice had to push past gravel in his chest.

"I don't care about the money. I don't want it. We both have what we really wanted from this marriage." She clicked her phone and gazed at it again. The yearning in her face was too acute to bear.

She didn't have what she wanted. Not really.

"Calli—"

"I have to leave before I get hurt, Stavros. Before I start believing I belong here and that you and I have more than sexual attraction. Before I fall in love with you."

He flinched at the word again, part of him thinking, *Do it. Fall.* But he couldn't say it aloud. Couldn't ask that of her. Couldn't accept it, even if she offered it.

"Take pity on me," she begged softly, touching his hand in a caress that made all the hairs on his body stand up. "I'm not as strong as you are."

Was that what he was? Strong? He felt weak as a kitten. Utterly helpless.

Very slowly, very reluctantly, he released his hold on her and let his empty hands hang between his knees.

"Whatever you want," he said in a rasp.

An hour later, she had packed a single bag and the apartment was empty. She was gone.

CHAPTER TEN

"WHAT THE HELL do you mean, she's gone?" Edward Michaels demanded a week later, when he called Stavros to the town house, apparently planning to hand over this mansion to his grandson as a belated wedding gift.

"I mean she left. Went back to Greece." Stavros stuffed his hands into his pockets and rocked his heels on the carpet where he had taken more stinging lectures from this old man than either of them could possibly recount.

"What the hell did you do?"

"Nothing." Stavros looked to the reds and golds he knew so well, bit the bullet and came clean. "I only married her to get the company."

"Yes, I know that," his grandfather said scathingly. "But why did you let her go?"

Of course his grandfather had seen clear through it. He was sharp as a tack.

"There's this thing called 'unlawful confinement.' Even I have my limits."

"Steven—"

"Don't call me that."

"Damn you, what does it matter what I call you?" Edward's hand slapped the antique desk that was pure decoration now. No longer used by that man, and would remain unused because Stavros couldn't stomach moving into this mansion and living here alone. He would rather be in the penthouse, where he could still see her rising to greet him, or walking up the stairs with a flash of her legs, or inviting him with a glance over her shoulder into the bed they had shared.

"*Imbecile*. All I have ever wanted was for you to quit throwing away your life like it doesn't matter and you do *this*?"

"I didn't throw her away. She *left*."

"Because you didn't hold on to her!"

"I *couldn't*! She deserves better. You think I don't know what matters? I was thinking of *her*."

"The hell you were. Are you feeling good, wallowing in the misery you created for yourself? I thought it was bad when you kept trying to kill yourself as punishment. Now you're going to carve out your heart and let her take it back to Greece?"

"It's where I left it," Stavros ground out.

"Your father would have wanted—"

"Don't tell me what he wanted. I know what he wanted." *Swim. I'll be right behind you.*

"He would have wanted you to live, Stavros. Properly. Not with a death wish. He would want you to love and have a family. Children. That's what *I* wanted for *him*. It's what I have always wanted for *you*."

"You wanted him to come back here and grow the company," Stavros reminded hotly. "You fought all the time about his staying in Greece."

"I wanted my son in my life. I wanted him back here to work with me, yes. I was creating a legacy and wanted him to be part of it. But I was..." Edward made a noise and waved a dismissive hand. "I was jealous. All right? Of your mother's hold on him. Your grandmother was a good woman, but I didn't love her the way your father loved your mother. I grew up a son of immigrants. We had nothing when we started. Money and success were always more important to me than love. I thought he should feel the same."

Stavros thought back to the latent anger in his father's voice, his mother's mollifying tone as they talked about the power struggle between the two generations. The conflict of loyalties.

"I regret that I was so hard on him for putting his wife and children ahead of me. I resented his buying a home in Greece and spending so much time with you there. I will always be sorry that he died before we resolved that. It was worse when you came to live here. I learned what a truly generous and loving person your mother is. They should have had more time together."

Stavros winced.

"I'm not blaming you for that! I'm telling you I blame myself. I shouldn't have made him feel as if he had to choose. You don't own the patent on being hardheaded, Stavros. We're all guilty of it. If I had asked him, rather than ordered, you might have been on an airplane to come here, rather than on the sea that day."

Stavros shook his head. "I'm the one who wanted to go fishing. It was my fault we were out there."

"And he indulged you because he wanted a better relationship with his son than he'd had with his father. It took me a long time to see that. To recognize the mistakes I had made with him and continued to make with you."

"You had every right to be hard on me. I was a little bastard."

"You were," Edward agreed without compunction. "And when you showed up with Calli the way you did, I saw myself in that cutthroat tactic. I realized I had raised you to be exactly like me, and I was not proud of myself. Then I got to know her and she doesn't give a damn about our money. The way she looked at you… Even I could recognize it as the furthest thing from avarice. She loves you. And, damn it, as much as you wanted the directorship, you left by five every night. You wanted to get back to her. I thought you were finding the kind of happiness I denied your father."

Stavros pinched the bridge of his nose, thinking about how he had watched the clock, eager to get home to his wife. Since she had left, time crawled. He worked late and woke early in an empty bed. It was a meaningless way to start a day.

Do you love me?

He had never felt he deserved such a thing. He

had certainly done his best to make his grand-father reject him. Only his mother and sisters were allowed to love him, and then only because he couldn't bear to hurt them by cutting them from his life.

Calli wasn't allowed to love him.

But when she had said her little speech about showing her love for her son by bowing out of his life, Stavros had known he had to let her go. He had been so certain he was doing right by her. Letting her go because he *loved* her.

"I am an imbecile."

"Finally we agree on something." His grand-father slapped his shoulder. "Go get her, son."

The knock at the door had Ophelia sitting up from her slouch on the sofa. "Pizza!" She clicked to pause the movie.

"You did not order pizza," Calli protested. She was going to gain three hundred pounds before this girl left for school.

Ophelia's expression blanked. "I thought you did."

"No. I said we're not charging anything more to your father's card."

"He's fine with it." Ophelia groaned, pushing

to her feet and sending Calli a scowl of impatience. It turned to a frown of curiosity. "If not pizza, who's at the door?" She moved to go on tiptoe, peering through the peephole. "Oh, my God!" she hissed. "It's your *husband*."

"What? Don't—"

Too late. Ophelia swung the door open. "*Geia*. What are you doing here?"

"Ophelia…" *Don't be rude*, Calli wanted to say, but the sight of Stavros nearly knocked her off her feet as she tried to stand. How could he have grown more handsome in a handful of weeks? While wearing stubble and a wrinkled shirt with a loosened tie?

At the sound of her voice, his gaze swept to slam into hers. "What are *you* doing *here*?"

"Girls' night," Ophelia volunteered with a wave at the litter they had accumulated. "Popcorn. Ice cream. Movie without nudity because she thinks I'm still *nine*." She folded her arms and lifted her brows in disdain.

Stavros came into the flat and closed the door.

"I mean, why are you staying here?" He didn't take his eyes off Calli. "I gave you the codes to our flat before you left." For the Xenakis penthouse, he meant. The one that provided views of both the Acropolis and the horizon on the sea, rather than being tucked on the edge of that posh address and overlooking the red lower rooftops of middle-class districts in Athens.

"Takis had to travel. Ophelia didn't want to stay with her grandparents." And their marriage was a farce. He was divorcing her. Had he forgotten? She hadn't.

"So he's not here?" Stavros cut a swift, sharp look around what had always seemed a luxurious flat to Calli, but compared to the way Stavros lived was only very nice. There were three bedrooms, but they were quite small. The decor was professionally selected, but the wall art was prints, not originals. The rugs weren't hand-loomed.

"He'll be gone the week. Why? Do you need to speak to him?"

"No. You're not working for him again, are you?"

"Kind of." She scratched her elbow. "I took his things to the dry cleaners and brought in some groceries, so I'm not freeloading. Mostly I just wanted to spend some time with Ophelia before she goes to school."

She had told Ophelia about Dorian. All of it. Ophelia was at an age where boys were beginning to occupy a lot of her thoughts, and it had seemed a sensible cautionary tale. It had also been cathartic, and Ophelia's reaction, so defensive on Calli's behalf, had been incredibly sweet. The empty calories and mindless movies had been Ophelia's attempt to spoil her, trying to help her heal while Calli figured out her next moves.

"We're homesick," Ophelia announced, moving to throw her arm around Calli. "I wanted her to take me back to the island, since technically she's still your wife and owns half of our old house, but she said it wouldn't be right." Ophelia wrinkled her nose at him. "Care to weigh in with a different opinion?"

"You may use the house anytime," Stavros offered with an offhand shrug.

"See?" Ophelia beamed smugly at Calli.

"If you could give us a few minutes of privacy right now."

"Oh." The girl's smile fell away. "Fine. I'll go

to my room and put in my earbuds so you grown-ups can talk."

Don't go, Calli wanted to say as Ophelia went down the hall and a door firmly closed. She wasn't prepared for this. She had convinced herself she would never see Stavros again.

And she had felt like she was slowly bleeding out because of it.

"Calli—you don't have to work." He touched his forehead, pained, adding impatiently, "Of course, you don't know that because you're not at the penthouse. If you were, you would have received the courier envelope from Norma, explaining that the Underwoods have made you a settlement offer. For what it's worth, Brandon will have to give up his own babies—those precious horses of his—to even approach the number I suggested was a good opener."

"What?"

"Do not sign anything until you discuss it with me or Takis. You sell yourself way too short in these kinds of things. Soak him, damn it. Give it all to charity after, if you can't stand to take it, but wring him dry."

He sounded positively bloodthirsty. "Is that why you're here? To discuss that? Because—"

"No." He frowned. "I'm here because..."

"Oh, were there other papers I should have signed?" Something worse occurred. "Your grandfather didn't back out, did he? Oh, Stavros—"

"Calli, be quiet." He ran a hand down his face, then held out his palm as if requesting patience. "I shouldn't be snapping at you. It's frustration. You weren't answering my texts and you weren't at the flat. Until I actually clapped eyes on you, I was quite worried something had happened."

"I'm fine. I changed my number when I got a new phone, but my email is still the same. You could have tried that."

"Why did you change your phone? I can afford to keep paying your bills. I told you to use our flat." He was back to snapping.

"It's your family's flat. It didn't seem right."

"It's *ours*. Yours and mine." He stared at her, lips a white line. "I'm not used to being erased from a person's life like this."

Was that hurt in his tone? She dropped her gaze

to his polished shoes. "You did a lot for me. I didn't want to keep taking advantage."

"I paid to have *one* letter written. You're not even wearing the clothes I bought for you. You left the necklace. Everything." Both his empty hands came up, like he couldn't fathom it.

She became acutely aware of her oversize T-shirt and striped leggings, her bare face and feet, the hair she had let air dry after her shower. Her lack of a bra.

She folded her arms.

"Do you love Takis? Is that it?"

"What? No. I told you. I love him like a father or a brother, not like that."

"Do you love *me*?"

"What?" She had the feeling of a hot spotlight finding her and glaring mercilessly, giving her no place to hide.

He knew. Behind his frustration was a glittering knowledge. Certainty. He was nodding like it was a foregone conclusion.

Her eyes stung and she looked away. "Stavros," she protested weakly.

"You do. You love me 'like that,' but you won't

let *me* take care of you. That doesn't make sense, Calli."

"You don't love me." The words came out thin and dry.

"You're completely content to love in one direction. You love your son without his even knowing you're alive. You love that girl even though she pushes all your buttons." He pointed toward the hall. "I would bet my entire fortune that deep down, you still have something like love for your parents, even though they don't deserve it. You love unconditionally and without reserve, Calli. And you love me. I know you do. But you left me and I finally figured out why. It's because there's one person you *don't* love. *Yourself.*"

She flinched as though he had struck her and started to turn away, but he caught her back, his hands warm and strong on her arms.

"It wasn't your fault, Calli."

"Don't." She tried to twist out of his hold, but he made her look him in the eye.

"Stop blaming yourself. You think I don't understand? I'm a piece of walking garbage. That's how I've felt since I outswam my father and made it to shore without him. You asked me if I loved you and I couldn't bring myself to saddle you with this." He tapped the place over his heart. "Who could possibly *want* my love? It's worthless."

"Don't say that."

"I let you go, didn't I? I let you walk away thinking I didn't love you. That you weren't worthy of love. You are. So very much. My love for you takes up so much room in me, I can barely breathe."

"Stavros."

"You're not tainted. You're not a bad mother. You're a warm and loving woman." He cupped her cheeks, filled her vision with the tender look on his face. "Redeem us both, Calli. Tell me I'm worthy of love and let me do the same for you."

Her vision began to blur. She blinked. The hot drops of her tears leaked onto her cheeks. "I've made a lot of mistakes."

"Me, too. But I love you exactly as you are. Now admit you love me, flaws and all."

"I do. I love you." The words hurt, tearing a hole in her heart that immediately filled in a rush, swelling it to painful capacity. She could hardly draw breath, especially when his lips touched hers.

The light kiss was benediction. A cool satin ribbon of touch, then a warmer press. Love. Sweet, sweet love that gently opened to passion. His hand moved into her hair. She stepped into his heat. Their mouths melded, deepening the kiss by increments until they were one being, sharing themselves with the other.

On and on they kissed. Her arms were around his neck, his heart beating so hard in his chest she felt it against her breast.

He drew back to dry her cheek with the pad of his thumb. *"S'agapó gynaíka mou."* *I love you, my wife.* "I refuse to divorce you. What do you think of that?"

"I think you're saving me from myself." She tucked her face into his shirt and hugged him tightly. "I'm scared to love this much. To want."

"I've thrown myself off cliffs with less terror than I felt coming after you. Failure was not an option." His hand clenched in her hair. "I told you once that I didn't have a reason to live, but I do. *You* are that reason, Calli." His arms banded her to him like he would never let her go.

"You have a lot of reasons, Stavros."

"You have a lot of modesty, *glykia mou*. Do not underestimate what you mean to me."

She drew back, the vastness of it all lodging in her chest. "I wanted to be pregnant," she admitted huskily, laying bare her deepest longing. It was a small test, perhaps, but he passed, easily.

"I wanted that, too." He caressed her jaw. "When you're ready, *agápi mou*. When you're sure of me, we will make as many babies as you want. And we will always have room for your son."

How did she deserve him? Her face crumpled. "I love you, Stavros."

"I love you, too."

EPILOGUE

OF ALL THE death-defying stunts Stavros had pulled over the years, nothing had left him as keyed up with adrenaline as watching his wife give birth. He'd been utterly helpless, forced to watch her suffer the pain and conquer her fear and push through a feat devised by nature as the ultimate test.

She and his son had come through with flying colors, but ten days later, Stavros was still dry-mouthed and quite certain he would never try *that* again.

"Is he awake?" Calli murmured drowsily, stirring from her nap on their bed.

Stavros looked from the growing discontent in the face of their swaddled infant to his wife. Her color was good, her smile well rested. Joy shone from beneath her heavy eyelids. She was so beautiful, she flipped his heart.

"He woke a little while ago, but has been trying to latch on to my arm the last few minutes. I thought I'd better bring him to the source. Company will be here soon anyway."

He sat on the edge of the bed and used his free hand to help her sit up. He waited while she arranged a few pillows and sat back, then handed over Lethe, watching as she took him to her breast as though she'd been doing this all her life.

He stole a slow, shaky breath. The boy didn't even weigh eight pounds, but the heft of responsibility he had thrown onto Stavros was profound. He was still coming to terms with it.

"Did I hear the phone earlier?"

"Ophelia. Exams went well. She's flying to Athens tomorrow and Takis will bring her next week. Then I talked to Takis and told him we'd like her to stay the summer if he's willing. He said at her age, extended time with a newborn could go either way in terms of curbing impulsive behavior."

They both chuckled and Stavros cocked his ear. "There's the doorbell."

Simpson would get it. They had settled into Edward's mansion last year, once her pregnancy had been confirmed, and had quickly adopted his grandfather's routine of spending half their time here and the rest at Galíni. In fact, they had gone there straight from the hospital and had only come back to the city last night.

Stavros went to greet their guests while Calli finished nursing, then made herself presentable.

When she came down the stairs, James—whom she still called Dorian in her heart—was hanging off the newel post at the bottom, waiting with barely contained impatience. His wide grin was missing all four front teeth. He extended a stuffed bear wearing a blue ribbon around its neck.

"Is that for me?" She stooped for a hug.

"It's for my brother." He was reaching the age where shows of affection were brief, even with his mothers, but he lingered in her looped arm, staring into Lethe's sleeping face. "Is that him?"

"This is Lethe, yes. He'll love it. Thank you." She tucked the bear against Lethe's freshly swaddled chest. "How is your sister? How was her appointment yesterday?"

"She's sick. She couldn't come."

"Just a cold," Wanda quickly provided as Calli shot her a look of concern. "Her counts were exactly where they should be." She crossed her fingers. "But we didn't want to get Lethe sick, so she stayed home with Daddy."

"I hope she feels better soon." Calli rose to hug Wanda.

Wanda smiled at Lethe with the melting expression most women wore when they gazed on a newborn. "Oh, he's beautiful. Look at that mouth. It's yours, same as James's."

They had become fast friends, she and Wanda. Calli had only been back in New York a few weeks when Wanda had invited her to visit James. She was a woman with a strong conscience who had been torturing herself since asking Calli to back off. "You obviously love him," she had said. "Who am I to deny my son more love in his life? What if something happened and I had kept you apart?"

Calli had sat with Wanda more than once as she waited for her daughter to come out of treatment. They shared a son and so much more.

"We've been very excited all morning," Wanda said ruefully, as James went on his tiptoes, trying to see Lethe again.

"Lethe, too." Stavros was completely straight-faced as he teased James. "He's been asking for you. All morning."

"He's a baby!" James protested, giving Stavros a you-can't-fool-me look.

Those two had their own special relationship characterized by discussions of heavy equipment and debates about superheroes and spirited wrestling matches over possession of a foam football.

"Do you want to hold him?" Calli sat down on the sofa and patted the cushion beside her. James wriggled his bottom into position beside her, right up against her side.

Her heart melted every time she was with him, every time she gazed into his bright, cheeky expression.

Gently she set her newborn son in the arms of her firstborn, keeping one hand lightly on the infant, securing him on James's lap. She was so happy in that moment, she could hardly bear it.

Lethe yawned and opened his eyes, making James jolt with excitement. "He's looking at me."

"He is." Her throat was nearly too tight to speak. "Say hello."

"Hello, Lethe. I'm James. Your brother." Then he leaned down to whisper. "I love you."

Calli's eyes filled.

"This is too cute for words," Wanda said, voice

throbbing with emotion. "Stavros, sit down with them. I need a photo."

He sat on the far side of James, arm outstretched so his fingers caressed Calli's shoulder. She lifted her gaze from her children to meet her husband's warm, dark eyes. She saw so much love reflected back at her, she thought she would combust.

"Do you know how happy it makes me to see you this happy?" he said in a quiet rumble.

"You must be pretty happy, then," she choked.

He gave her cheek an affectionate brush with the back of his finger, sweeping away her tear. "I am."

Later, when the house was quiet and their son was settled in his bassinet, and they were naked in the big bed they shared, she snuggled into Stavros and said with a tiny throb of old anxiety, "I sometimes wonder what would have happened if Sebastien hadn't sent you to the island."

Sebastien was still setting up his extreme challenges, but Stavros was picking and choosing, just as happy to schedule a ski trip or another more mainstream vacation with his friends. Calli had developed wonderful friendships with all the wives, which was another thing she would have missed if Stavros hadn't taken that dare from his friend.

The happiness she enjoyed seemed so tentative sometimes.

But his low rumble was reassuringly confident. "You would have come here for Dorian and I would have seen you. We would be exactly where we are right now."

"In a city this huge?" She lifted her head from his shoulder, trying to see him in the dim light from the clock. "You really believe you would have noticed me?"

"I do. Even if you had been able to keep him, our lives would have found another way to intersect. We were meant to be together, Calli."

"Oh." His words panged her heart. "When you say things like that, I believe you." She cuddled into him again, squeezing her arm across his waist, eyes closed against emotive tears.

"No one could love you the way I love you." He cradled her close, lips against her hair, then her cheekbone, searching for her mouth. "No one else could love me the way you do."

They kissed. The passion between them hadn't abated, staying strong between them right up to the evening before she delivered. He'd been a perfect gentleman since the birth, but she could feel how aroused he became, and stroked him.

He groaned. "I miss making love to you."

"We'll have to find other ways to appease ourselves, won't we?" she teased. "Lucky for you, I'm an inventive woman."

"I'm fairly innovative myself. Let's see what we come up with."

He pressed over her and she made a noise of indulgence, already sinking into the world of pleasure he gave her. The joy.

He was right. Something this perfect must have been fated. She never worried about it again.

* * * * *

If you enjoyed the second part of
THE SECRET BILLIONAIRES *trilogy,*
don't forget to read the first installment!

DI MARCELLO'S SECRET SON
by Rachael Thomas
Available now!

And, coming November 2017,
SALAZAR'S ONE-NIGHT HEIR
by Jennifer Hayward.

MILLS & BOON®
Large Print – October 2017

Sold for the Greek's Heir
Lynne Graham

The Prince's Captive Virgin
Maisey Yates

The Secret Sanchez Heir
Cathy Williams

The Prince's Nine-Month Scandal
Caitlin Crews

Her Sinful Secret
Jane Porter

The Drakon Baby Bargain
Tara Pammi

Xenakis's Convenient Bride
Dani Collins

Her Pregnancy Bombshell
Liz Fielding

Married for His Secret Heir
Jennifer Faye

Behind the Billionaire's Guarded Heart
Leah Ashton

A Marriage Worth Saving
Therese Beharrie

MILLS & BOON®
Large Print – November 2017

The Pregnant Kavakos Bride
Sharon Kendrick

The Billionaire's Secret Princess
Caitlin Crews

Sicilian's Baby of Shame
Carol Marinelli

The Secret Kept from the Greek
Susan Stephens

A Ring to Secure His Crown
Kim Lawrence

Wedding Night with Her Enemy
Melanie Milburne

Salazar's One-Night Heir
Jennifer Hayward

The Mysterious Italian Houseguest
Scarlet Wilson

Bound to Her Greek Billionaire
Rebecca Winters

Their Baby Surprise
Katrina Cudmore

The Marriage of Inconvenience
Nina Singh

017 Rom LP

MILLS & BOON®

Why shop at millsandboon.co.uk?

Each year, thousands of romance readers find their perfect read at millsandboon.co.uk. That's because we're passionate about bringing you the very best romantic fiction. Here are some of the advantages of shopping at www.millsandboon.co.uk:

* **Get new books first**—you'll be able to buy your favourite books one month before they hit the shops

* **Get exclusive discounts**—you'll also be able to buy our specially created monthly collections, with up to 50% off the RRP

* **Find your favourite authors**—latest news, interviews and new releases for all your favourite authors and series on our website, plus ideas for what to try next

* **Join in**—once you've bought your favourite books, don't forget to register with us to rate, review and join in the discussions

Visit **www.millsandboon.co.uk** for all this and more today!